Table of Co

5 Lesbian Steamy FF Explicit..................................
Lesbian BDSM Mistress Romance ....
CHAPTER 1 9
CHAPTER 2 13
CHAPTER 3 17
CHAPTER 4 21
CHAPTER 5 25
CHAPTER 6 29
Virgin Lesbian Friend Seduction 33
CHAPTER 1 37
CHAPTER 2 41
CHAPTER 3 45
CHAPTER 4 49
CHAPTER 5 53
CHAPTER 6 57
Lesbian Virgin Friend Seduction 2 61
CHAPTER 1 65
CHAPTER 2 69
CHAPTER 3 73
CHAPTER 4 77
CHAPTER 5 81
CHAPTER 6 85
Naughty Wife Lesbian Experience 89
CHAPTER 1 93
CHAPTER 2 97
CHAPTER 3 101
CHAPTER 4 105
Naughty Hotwife Swingers Experience 111
CHAPTER 1 115
CHAPTER 2 119
CHAPTER 3 123
CHAPTER 4 127

5 Lesbian Steamy FF Explicit

Sexy Short Erotic Stories
Taboo Frist Time Forbidden Hot FFF Threesome Menage

Adult Naughty Sex Erotica Romance Seduction Fiction
P.KITTY

Kindle Edition
Copyright 2021 Khelan Publishing
Published by Khelan Publishing
License Notes: This ebook is licensed for your personal enjoyment only. This ebook may not be re-sold or given away to other people. If you would like to share this ebook with another person, please purchase an additional copy for each person you share it with. If you're reading this book and did not purchase it, or it was not purchased for your use only, then you should return and purchase your own copy. Thank you for respecting the hard work of this author.
Khelan Publishing Printing March 2021
5 4 3 2 1

~

All characters in this book have no existence outside the imagination of the author and have no relation whatsoever to anyone bearing the same name or names. They are not even distantly inspired by any individual known or unknown to the author, and all incidents are pure inventions of fiction.

Lesbian BDSM Mistress Romance

Sexy FF Short Sex Story
(First Time Female Taken by Dominating Escort)

Adult Erotic Seduction Fiction
LISA LICKITTY

Kindle Edition
Copyright 2021 Khelan Publishing
Published by Khelan Publishing
License Notes: This ebook is licensed for your personal enjoyment only. This ebook may not be re-sold or given away to other people. If you would like to share this ebook with another person, please purchase an additional copy for each person you share it with. If you're reading this book and did not purchase it, or it was not purchased for your use only, then you should return and purchase your own copy. Thank you for respecting the hard work of this author.
Khelan Publishing Printing March 2021
5 4 3 2 1

~

All characters in this book have no existence outside the imagination of the author and have no relation whatsoever to anyone bearing the same name or names. They are not even distantly inspired by any individual known or unknown to the author, and all incidents are pure inventions of fiction.

Table of Content

Lesbian BDSM Mistress Romance

> CHAPTER 1
> CHAPTER 2
> CHAPTER 3
> CHAPTER 4

CHAPTER 1

I walk through the hallway of Dad's building to his office. He's the owner of Ink and Quill Publishing House, an up-and-coming publisher that's been getting better and better work over the last eight years.

Right before the divorce between Dad and Mom, he opened up the publishing house and I remember the extra stress and fights that came as a result of the workload on his plate. It revealed another side of both my parents and at fifteen, I watched them walk away from each other.

Shaking my head free of that thought, I knock on the door in front of me until I'm told to come in. Dad looks up at me and arches an eyebrow as he pauses. "Rebecca! How is my favorite assistant editor?"

"I better be your favorite, considering you trained me." I tease.

Dad chuckles, that sparkle coming back into his dark eyes. I sit in one of the mildly comfortable chairs in front of his desk and give him the list of stories that have been approved by all the assistant editors – a more condensed amount than have applied to us.

"Here are the stories ready for the last round of edits or to be cut as the editor in chief approves. There's also notes about each story including potential ways they can be marketed and the demographic it would appeal to." I say, trying to stay all business.

Dad took me under his wing when I chose to stay with him instead of leaving with mom, but I had to earn my place here just like anyone else. At twenty, as a senior in college, I started my internship and it became a real job by the time I finished grad school at twenty-two. It's been two months, but I still feel like I'm proving myself over and over again so no one can say that I only got the job because Dad's the owner and boss.

"You're on top of things, just like I've come to expect." He says before folding his hands in front of him. "What did you think about the invitation I sent you?"

"I don't know what good I can do at a fundraising event."

"I'd like you to be there. I can help you meet others. You know I want you to run the company someday and the sooner we get your name out there the easier that will be in the future." He shrugs. "If you don't feel ready, that's fine. We can wait."

But I notice that slight little tug down on his lips. This is important to him. I know that. He's trying to include me in the life he's been building while I've been at school. Before the divorce I was a daddy's girl. I clung to him, saw him as the hero the world needed, but then he was launching a business and I was working on doing every club, every bit of volunteering and extra work I could do to try and keep my parents happy and off to college.

Time has gone fast and I know that he wants this opportunity to bring us closer together. I chew my bottom lip as he looks over the list I provided to him. He highlights a few and sets it to the side, raising his eyes to look at me.

"What is it, Becca?"

"I don't really have anything to wear to an event like this. Can I do like slacks and a nice shirt or is a dress mandatory?" I whisper.

He beams, lighting up the whole office with his dimpled smile. "Black tie optional which means you are more than welcome to wear slacks and a nice top. You can probably combine the two tonight."

"Okay. Then ... I'll see you there!" I agree. "Unless you want to get lunch today?"

"I have to work through lunch, honey. But I'm very excited to share tonight with you. My own daughter a rising start in the industry."

"If only I was a writer." I tease.

He chuckles. "You and me both."

The day passes in a haze of reading and then I'm home getting ready. I turn in front of my phone camera, showing my best friend the high waisted slacks, I have and the off the shoulder, airy, white top I have. It compliments my black hair and with some red lipstick I think it looks nice.

Kylie shakes her head. "Okay, add a black belt to pull the fabric in so it shows off your curves."

"My dad is going to be there, Ky."

"Yeah, well, so will other bachelors. Eligible bachelors." She points at me. "And bachelorettes."

I groan and get the belt, securing it high on my waist. It does bring out my figure. My hips are wide and I have thick thighs, but smaller boobs. It does look nicer now though. I chew my bottom lip and glance to Kylie.

"It's not too ..."

"An outfit isn't going to out you, Becca. I thought you were bisexual and proud?" She leans her head to the side.

"Yeah, well. It hasn't ever come up with dad. I don't really care about anyone else's opinion." I say surely, then brush through my hair again. "I'll add some heels and it'll be fine."

"You got this, babes." Kylie assures with her thumbs up before looking to the side. "Shit, I have to go! Tell me all about it later!"

"I will." I promise, then end our call.

One more look in the mirror, a glance at the time, and I'm rushing to get to the venue. I show my invitation to the person in the front and I'm ushered inside. I recognize no one, but I learned quickly how to fake being comfortable. It's never been hard.

I still want to find Dad though, to show that I'm here. After weaving through people, I see him, with a younger woman on his arm. And just like that, every bit of professionalism is forgotten.

CHAPTER 2

She's so beautiful that I feel like my jaw is on the floor – cartoon style. My dad kisses the top of her head which is a whole other roller coaster. The woman has long flowing blonde hair that's perfectly done so it rolls with her curves. And she definitely has curves on her lithe body. Her face is sharp, high cheek bones, firm lips, and icy gray eyes.

The dress she wears is red and clings to her, plunging between her breasts while still somehow pushing them up. She's so perfect I can imagine her as the muse for Aphrodite statues, but she's real and her eyes flick to me as I approach, taking me in slowly.

"Dad." I greet him.

She looks between us then nods to me politely. Dad loops his arm with hers and smiles. "Rebecca, this is Kira. My date for this evening."

"Nice to meet you." I nod, suddenly feeling utterly unremarkable and under dressed. Maybe I should have gone for something with more flair.

"And you." There's a bit of an accent on her tongue, but I'm not sure what it is.

I do know that my brain has fully disconnected from my mouth. Dad sweeps me up, introducing me to others as his daughter, assistant editor, crediting me with four of the top publications that have come out in the last month.

I don't back down, don't show any distraction ... or I try not to, but after an hour, I'm exhausted. There are so many faces and names in my head and none of them are connecting. I sit in a chair set up by a wall and exhale slowly.

Just as I'm starting to calm down and playing an internal matching game for names and faces Kira approaches. Her hips sway as she walks and her heels click on the floor. She has to know how she captivates a room, how effortlessly she can steal every bit of attention without saying a word.

She sits next to me and shakes her head. "Such events – they feel so long with so many people."

Russian. Definitely a Russian accent. And the way her lips move when she speaks is downright entrancing. She's so far beyond beautiful that my brain just sizzles at her proximity. I blink a few times and realize she's talking to me when her cold eyes take me in.

"You are Jack's daughter, yes?"

"Yes." I jump slightly. "Sorry. I'm overwhelmed. I'm not usually so quiet or ... off."

Kira pats my hand gently. "It will be easier. After a few months, it feels normal. Only remember the important names." Then she leans towards me. "And ask for business cards."

I laugh. "Really? Is that a good method to remember?"

"So many people have them!" She says as she leans towards me. "And you are pretty, so they will share them quickly. Especially the writers. They want an in and will give anything you could ask."

I know she's with my dad, but her calling me pretty has electricity buzzing through my skin at such an intense voltage, I feel frazzled and calm at the same time. Kira looks around and shakes her head.

"Not enough women here."

I look around and notice the same, then shrug. "That means we should stick together, not just because you're dating my dad."

"Date is ... is a strong word." She smiles slightly. "I come to events with him. It can be interesting, but not always fun."

"What do you do for work? What do you consider fun?"

Kira smiles and leans back. "I am a translator. Russian to English. I work though universities. Parties can be fun, with the right people. I like art, books, staying home and reading with a glass of wine."

"That sounds like a much better night." I chuckle, then shake my head. "But don't tell my dad I said that. I think he really wants me to enjoy this kind of thing. Or at least enjoy it enough that I could do it alone in a few years."

"You like working in publishing?"

"Well, I really like writing, but as much as I like it, I feel like I don't have a story to tell yet, or not the right story. Anytime I sit down, I can only get a few sentences or words down and then I realize how little I have to say. What could I possibly say that hasn't already been said?"

Kira taps her bottom lip. "I think, everyone has a different life. Even if some things are the same, if people can relate to the story, they'll want to read it. Then they'll feel less alone."

I blink at her. "That's amazing."

She grins. "I will get us drink and we can hide here until it's time to dance."

"My dad might miss you." I say before she leaves. "I understand if you have to shake hands or spend time with him instead."

Kira looks over where my dad is happily talking with about four other guys. "I think we could have more fun. I'd rather talk than listen to compliments and then have basics explained."

"Ah, man-splaining. I can save you from that." I assure.

She smiles, her gray eyes thawing a little. I wait for her in the same spot and she returns with a red wine that's delicious. And then we spend the entire party together, talking literature, getting to know each other, and laughing at some of the guests while trying not to offend anyone. We even play a game where we fill in conversations for people that are off to the sides.

By the time my dad collects us to leave, I feel invigorated and ... half in love with my dad's date. When he kisses her, a pang of jealousy shoots through me, but I smile, tell Kira what a great time I had and promise to text dad when I get home.

He opens the door for Kira, then meets my eyes. "What do you think?"

I don't know if he means about her or the party, but I smile. "I think I could get used to this."

CHAPTER 3

Memories of Kira still sizzle and crackle across my skin when I get home. I look myself over and decide I definitely need to make an effort to dress up at the next event, which dad told me will be in another two weeks.

I won't see Kira until then which is a special kind of torture. And since I have no work to do tonight, all I can think about is her eyes, her gentle lips, the way she'd touch me to keep my attention, innocent little brushes across my knee, my shoulder, my hand.

She'd clutch me tighter as we wound through the crowd like she didn't want to lose me. It's new. Most people, men or women, grab me by a shirt or don't care if we get separated. But she held onto me like it was the most natural thing to do and halfway through the night it felt more like she was my date than my dad's. Which I'm not complaining about either.

I slowly stroke down my shirt, following the curve of my breasts until I reach my belt. I pull it off and close my eyes, imagine Kira doing it. Slowly slipping my shirt off, I light a candle and rub over my chest, the thin bra I wear that doesn't hide how hard my nipples are.

Would she like touching me? Would she be gentle, or take control? Would she throw me on the bed and tear my pants off me so she could sink her fingers deep inside me and take what she wants, what we both want eagerly, quickly, or go slow?

Tonight, since we just met, I think it would be slow, so that's what I do. I strip myself down while letting my fingers linger in every sensitive space. I tease my nipples while thinking of her lips, imagining how they'd wrap around me, gently stroke my clit with my fingers while remembering how her hand would tighten on my thigh when any guy would look me over with a hungry gaze.

She's had me soaking wet all night and I'm realizing how wet I am right now. I bet she'd feel like this too, wet, warm, completely bare, perfect and ... and just touching her wouldn't be enough. I'd need to taste her too, make her moan, have her come.

And she'd do the same, licking my clit with her tongue, sucking gently, driving me more and more insane.

I gasp as I rub my fingers faster over my clit. "Oh, Kira."

Just before I come, I reach into my nightstand and pull out my vibrator. I rub it over my nipples, a good little warm up, then crank up the vibrations to slide it over my clit before thrusting it into my soaking pussy.

Between the toy, my fingers, and the fantasy of Kira being the one watching, touching, taking me, it doesn't take me long to come. I finish and pant, staring at the ceiling. As soon as I come down from the back arching orgasm, guilt hits me.

She made it clear that she and my dad aren't exclusive, but it's so wrong to fantasize about her. She's not mine. I don't even know if she likes girls ... but it doesn't hurt anyone does it? My little fantasies?

I clean up, lay in bed, and can't stop myself from thinking of how she smiled at me when she talked about writing, reading, me. I can't wait to see her again. Three weeks is going to feel so long.

But it flies by. Between work and so much going on with friends, I feel like I can't come up for air until I'm getting ready for the next event. I pull on a light blue silky dress. This one still isn't tight, but it's comfortable. It's a step forward, much better than slacks.

I lightly do my makeup and pin my hair so it shows I've made a little more of an effort. I'll let dad think it's for his colleagues, but I know it's for Kira. Even if I have no promise she'll be there, she's worth preparing for.

And over the next four months, the fundraisers and events become the highlight of my month. Kira is always there and we always end up talking, sometimes dancing, always laughing and smiling. We even dance.

Which means I always come home frustrated, with her on my mind with only my fingers and toys to take care of myself. I've been getting more and more riled. I've even flirted with her, masturbated in the traffic on the way home, and have at least six different plans on how to get her phone number to ask her to lunch or dinner or something innocent.

When I walk into a huge regional, invite only fundraiser, I adjust my white dress. It's a little tighter, shows my legs and some cleavage, but it's still classy. My black hair is curled, my lips done in a wine red, and I have on red heels, just because I know I can pull it off.

I even shaved for tonight. But I'm sure I'm going to go home alone again. Despite the numbers from men written on bar napkins, only one person makes me overflow with need and Kira always leaves with my dad.

It's okay though. I can handle it. Just like I handle myself when I get home, just like I reign myself in at the event. I can get through this event just like I've gotten through the others. No surprises, nothing out of the norm.

Because the fantasy is better than getting caught, right?

"Rebecca!" Kira squeezes me against her chest and I feel myself heat up. Her breasts press against mine and when she holds me away, her eyes sweep over my dress. "You are beautiful. More than anyone here deserves."

"Only half as beautiful as you."

She shakes her head, but takes my hand. "I've been waiting for you. You're the only way I get through these events."

Tonight might be harder than normal if this is how we're starting.

CHAPTER 4

Kira leans towards me and whispers in my ear, her breath brushes across my throat and I swear I feel her lips stroke across my ear. "You really are beautiful, Rebecca. Did you read that book I left for you?"

I did. It was so dirty, but beautiful and devastating at the same time. A work of art with erotica laced in. I swallow and turn my head. She's so close our noses almost brush. "I did. It was ... It was perfect, Kira. How did you find it?"

She smiles. "I translated it. I wasn't sure how well I did. You're the first person I showed."

"Kira, can I have this dance?" My dad asks, stealing her from me at the worst moment.

My heart is bursting. Kira smiles. "I'll be right back to pick your brain."

I smile, but my eyes stroke across Kira. The sexy black dress she wears is more than I can handle. It clings to her curves, shows the entirety of her back, so I know she's not wearing a bra, and the long slit up her thigh doesn't hide how muscular and soft her legs are. When my dad pulls her up, the neckline shifts, flashing the top curves of her breasts and I know right then and there I'm not going to make it until I get home.

My mind is reeling, picturing how easily I could push her dress down her body, wondering what would be waiting for me, the way her lips would part, how satiny her skin would feel under my fingers and how she'd be warm under my touch.

The second they're on the dance floor, I make a mad dash for the bathroom. I thought I'd be able to make it through tonight without any issue. I was so wrong.

I've had blinders on since I met Kira. Mr. or Mrs. right could walk into my life and I wouldn't see them. Not since I met her. She's so bright, so overwhelming, so ... perfect of me, checking every box and then some that I feel like everyone else is just a faceless member of the crowd when she's around.

I push open the bathroom door and then lean against it. The bathrooms here are luxurious. Only two stalls per bathroom, a plush couch, candles, low music, low lighting. They're classy and elegant and clean ... and empty. Exactly what I need.

I flick the lock, then go to one of the large bathroom stalls. I shut the door and pull my dress up and over my thighs. I close my eyes as I lean back against the wall. My fingers slowly rub up my thigh and I find my thong soaking wet.

Five minutes with Kira is all it takes for that reaction. I drag them down my legs, set them to the side and rub my pussy. I'm so turned on I know it won't take long. I circle my clit thinking of Kira, her icy eyes, her tempting body, the way she never hesitates to touch me, how she makes me feel like the only person in a room with a look or whisper.

"Oh, yes."

I'm so slick and warm and the pleasure slowly spreading across my nerves feels twice as naughty since I'm in a public bathroom. I pant and sink my fingers into my pussy. The wet sounds of my fingers pushing into my pussy over and over echo on the marble and I let out another low moan.

"So close. So-"

The stall door opens and I stare at Kira. I swallow, my fingers jerking away from my pussy as if that will make this experience better. I'm still standing in front of her with my dress bunched up, everything on display with my underwear off.

"Kira!"

She looks me over slowly, takes a step forward, then another, until she shuts the stall door behind her and locks it. I stare at her, confused, hot and bothered, my whole body humming with unfulfilled need. My knees shake as Kira reaches for my wet hand.

"Rebecca." She breathes slowly, then pulls my hand up.

I almost jerk away, wanting to wipe my fingers off on my dress or something to cut through the embarrassment, but Kira pulls my fingers to her mouth and licks the wetness from them. She lets out a harsh breath, then slides her lips around my fingers, sucking as her tongue teases me with quick little flicks.

Everything in me melts. My reason is gone, there's only Kira, her sharp gray eyes trained on my face as she sucks my fingers. Her mouth is hot, soft, wet and her lips tighten around my knuckle before she makes a soft sound in the back of her throat and closes her eyes.

She releases me with a soft pop and licks her bottom lip slowly. "Hmm. So sweet."

I can't stop myself and I wouldn't if I could. I've been craving Kira, this moment, her mouth since the moment I met her and if her licking my fingers after I used them to fuck myself doesn't make her feelings clear, then nothing else will.

Wrapping an arm around her waist, I pull her against me and kiss her hungrily, sucking her bottom lip and tasting myself on her. Our tongues tease and I moan, taking everything, I can from this moment.

I stroke down her neck with one hand while the other slides to her bottom. Our breasts push together and she licks across my tongue. Tasting my own juices on her mouth kills any lingering sanity in my head.

I need her.

Now.

CHAPTER 5

Kira pushes me back and kisses down my neck. "We need to take care of you."

I moan in response. She licks across my throat, then her fingers stroke over my mound. "You're so beautiful, Rebecca. So sweet. Better than any wine."

I whimper as her fingers slide across my clit. This is better than any of my fantasies. Her thin, delicate fingers working my clit like she knows just what I need to come, just what will push me over the edge is wile.

Another moan echoes in my throat and Kira kisses me hungrily before her fingers push into my pussy. I'd been fucking myself slow so I could stay quiet, but Kira's fingers are fast and demanding. Her face flushes as she licks across my bottom lip before she kisses me again.

But her fingers, so fast, hitting my g-spot every time until even my thighs feel wet makes it impossible to be quiet. I moan, turning my face to the side and Kira pants. "I've wanted to do this for so long, Rebecca."

"You have?" I ask.

Her fingers pump deeper inside me and my legs shake. She kisses my neck. "So long. Once won't be enough. Not even close."

I groan and grind down on her hand as she continues fingering me. She shakes her head and drops to her knees. "I can't wait."

"What?"

She kisses my hip, then licks along my slit. As she fucks me fast and hard with her fingers, teasing areas I don't think I've ever touched, her tongue circles my clit. It's such an intense combination, pleasure rips across my nerves, spreads across me with heat rolling in its wake, lapping at me like flames.

I know I'm not going to last long. There's no way.

My fingers knot in her hair and she pants. She sucks and licks across my clit, teasing me until I'm at the edge of my sanity, my reason, everything. I moan let my head fall back against the wall. My whole body shakes and then, when she flattens her tongue over my clit, I explode.

My knees give out and I fall into Kira's lap. She smiles, then kisses me hungrily. The taste of her and me on her mouth is too much. Our tongues massage and stroke each other as my hand strokes up the inside of her thigh. She's not wearing any underwear at all.

I tease her clit and find her dripping wet and so hot. She's so ready for me and I can't wait. Not when this moment is right here for us. Just as I'm about to push my fingers inside her, the door to the bathroom opens.

A girl giggles and I jerk away from Kira.

In a mad dash, we get dressed, but she steals my panties, dangling them in front of me before stuffing them in her purse. She takes my hand and we wash our hands, then she smiles.

"I'm stealing you. You're all mine for the night."

"You can just leave?"

"Of course." She winks at me. "But let's not let your dad in on this."

We make a mad dash for her car, running away like too over eager teenagers. She drives us to a townhouse and we can't make it up the stairs without kissing multiple times. She shoves me against the wall and wraps a leg around my hip as she devours my mouth.

I groan and rub up her thigh. I dig my nails into her ass and she shakes her head, murmuring something in Russian. The second we're inside her apartment, I push her onto the couch and lower myself to the floor. I need her, now.

Kira watches, holding my hair back as I lick and kiss up her thigh. I spread her legs, but she pushes me down to the floor. She grins at me, bites her lip, then straddles my face. I lick my bottom lip and nod.

"Do you want me, Rebecca?"

"More than anything!" I jerk her down so I can lick across her clit.

She tastes like salted honey. I moan and bury my face in her pussy, lapping at her clit while I finger her pussy from behind. Kira moans and rolls her hips across my tongue. I groan and lick her faster, harder. I don't have any patience and neither does she.

Kira uses my mouth eagerly, moaning and letting her dress fall over her shoulders until her breasts are free. They're perky, round, perfect.

I can't wait to touch and lick every inch of her. I've never wanted someone more, never wanted to please someone this much. I groan and suck her clit hard. It does her in. She gasps and my chin and lips are soaked. Kira's body jerks again, spasming as she rides out her orgasm.

Then she jerks me up and kisses me hard. I groan as she does and I let her drag me to another room. She shoves me down on the bed, pushes my dress up and tears it off me. Hers must have fallen on the way to her room because she's completely naked.

Kira strokes my breasts, cupping them and licking across my nipples one at a time while her icy eyes stay on me. "You are perfect." Another lick. "Sweet." Another. "Beautiful." She sucks on my nipples hard, teasing me with her teeth. "And all mine."

I groan and nod. Whatever she wants, I'm going to make sure she gets. Neither of us are going to forget tonight. Kira reaches under her bed and pulls out a box. She shows me a long dildo and grins at me.

"We have options. Many."

I nod. "I'm yours. Completely yours."

She groans and fits her mouth to mine again, her tongue working me into a frenzy so intense, I'm sure I'm going to come from making out alone.

"To better quality books and better-quality company." I agree.

We clink glasses, take a drink, then Kira shakes her head at me. "I wasn't even sure you'd be interested."

"And I thought you were just playing nice since I'm Jack's daughter."

She giggles and kisses me slowly. "Let me spend tonight proving otherwise."

I nod and she dives into the book, reading it slowly, with so much passion and a reading voice that I'd kill for. I feed her cheese and meat and let the wine, the sex, and her voice lull me to the best sleep I'll ever have with the hope that this won't be gone in the morning.

Kira's fingers push my hair away from my face. "Until the morning, sweet Becca."

I roll and cuddle her against me. "Then we try to shower without getting dirtier."

She giggles and I fall asleep with a smile on my face.

Virgin Lesbian Friend Seduction

FF Erotic Short Story
Sexy Frist Time Girl on Girl Hot Steamy Experience

Adult Romance Fiction
LISA LICKITTY

Kindle Edition
Copyright 2021 Khelan Publishing
Published by Khelan Publishing
License Notes: This ebook is licensed for your personal enjoyment only. This ebook may not be re-sold or given away to other people. If you would like to share this ebook with another person, please purchase an additional copy for each person you share it with. If you're reading this book and did not purchase it, or it was not purchased for your use only, then you should return and purchase your own copy. Thank you for respecting the hard work of this author.
Khelan Publishing Printing March 2021
5 4 3 2 1

5 LESBIAN STEAMY FF EXPLICIT SEXY SHORT EROTIC STORIES 35

~

All characters in this book have no existence outside the imagination of the author and have no relation whatsoever to anyone bearing the same name or names. They are not even distantly inspired by any individual known or unknown to the author, and all incidents are pure inventions of fiction.

Table of Content

Virgin Lesbian Friend Seduction

> CHAPTER 1
> CHAPTER 2
> CHAPTER 3
> CHAPTER 4
> CHAPTER 5
> CHAPTER 6

CHAPTER 1

Natasha nods to Rhea in the back corner of the library as their pinkies link. "If we haven't had sex by the time our last final comes and goes ...."

Rhea blushes fiercely and looks around. "Natasha, I- I agree to it, I just don't want to agree here, in the library. Someone is going to hear us and think we're crazy."

"It's college everyone is." Natasha waves that away, flipping her dark hair over her shoulder as her blue eyes focus entirely on Rhea. "Finish it."

Rhea sighs and nods, lowering her voice and talking so fast that if Natasha hadn't known her for the last four years, she probably wouldn't have understood it. "Then we'll have sex with each other so we don't leave college as virgins."

"Deal?" Natasha asks her pinky tight around Rhea's.

The blonde nods, still looking around like anyone else is going to be in the library at 1 am on a Friday. Natasha leans forward, with their pinkies still locked and kisses Rhea on the mouth. When she draws back, Rhea's blushing even more fiercely. "What was that?"

"Sealing the deal with a kiss," Natasha said.

"Better than sealing it in blood," Rhea adjusts her glasses, "Our final semester. I can't believe we're four months away from graduation."

"And four months away from kicking our V-cards."

They agree, quietly talking about who they hope it will be. If it'll be that quiet boy in Rhea's classes that always seems to show up in the library or hallway when she's alone. Would it be Natasha's crush – the T.A. from her anthropology class?

They promised each other they'd try harder to get laid, since they really hadn't put any effort into it. That's what this deal was all about – meant to light a fire under their asses so they'll actually go out and makes it clear that they want sex.

But as the semester chugs along, they go to fewer and fewer parties and end up so far, their books and job applications that they don't notice the counting down on the calendar. Only once the last day of April hits does Natasha even remember they made a pact to begin with, way back in January when they'd had to bundle up just to walk to the library.

She tries to find someone at the library, after all people have been known to hookup there and it's not like she's not pretty, her thick black hair, and her lean body with soft, tight curves. She had seen guys look at her plenty of times.

The only issue was that she didn't want to lose her virginity half drunk in some frat boy's musty car ... or musty room at that rate. She glances back at Rhea, blond with tan skin, more like a hippie than anyone she'd ever met, but with generous curves that she'd seen more than one guy whistle over.

But Rhea isn't a people person. It had taken a full two months for her to warm up to Natasha even though they'd been roommates. Natasha knows that getting her over the hurdle of having sex for the first time will be difficult mostly because of her own nature. Shame, she's sexy, has a ten out of ten, knock out body and is too afraid to take what she wants for fear of being rejected.

Natasha doesn't hate the idea of losing her virginity to her best friend. She can get the toys so it actually counts and no guy will be able to say otherwise. It's just a matter of knowing where to go and Natasha has plenty of ideas on that.

"Hey, Rhea," She murmurs, walking back to her friend. "Let's go somewhere today."

"We have finals to study for."

"I'm well aware. Neither of us are on the cusp of passing or failing with the final, so let's take a study break and take care of something else."

"Something else? Like what?" Rhea asks, standing up slowly, not saying no.

"Remember our deal?"

"When you're driving you pick the music?" She asks.

Natasha laughs and shakes her head. "Give me two hours. You'll remember our deal, we'll be all set, and then we can get back to studying if that's what you want to do."

"It is what I want to do, Tash. Can we just wait on whatever errand this is?"

"As if you don't know everything you need already to succeed. Come on, R. Give me this before we start counting down summer and then have to deal with what comes after college." Natasha pouts, sticking out her bottom lip and flashing her puppy dog eyes at Rhea.

Rhea scratches the back of her neck, and then gives in, like she always does. Natasha bounces and happily drags her from the library and to a local sex shop.

On the way, Natasha looks Rhea over. It definitely wouldn't be bad to lose her virginity to Rhea. Half the guys, at least, in school are less attractive than her and she's so sweet and careful.

She's normally in cut off shorts and some kind of 'save the planet' or knit top. A cute little flower child, that Natasha would be more than happy to touch and kiss, for the sake of the pact, of course. She's always been interested in guys and she knows that doesn't just change overnight ... right?

Shaking her head, she pushes Rhea to get out of the car as they joke around together. That joking comes to a dead stop when Rhea sees where they are. She turns her frustrated gaze on Natasha and arches an eyebrow.

"We're missing valuable study time for this?"

"We'll go in, buy some stuff for relaxing, and then get right back to it. I promise. Consider this ... preparation. Another way to learn about things that aren't taught in classes," Natasha takes her hands leading her towards the store.

"If I wanted to relax, I just would have grabbed something from my stash, Tash. I have plenty of pot."

"We're going to try a new way. Remember? If we're still virgins by the time we hit finals ..."

Rhea's eyes widen and she swallows hard. "I thought that was just a joke.

"Tough shit, it's not."

CHAPTER 2

Rhea just watches as Natasha shows her the different kind of dildos, vibrators, and toys in general. It's overwhelming. There's just so much to take in and Rhea can't exactly deal with how much new she's being forced to deal with.

Also, who the hell would want a toy that looks like a penis and is all veiny and ... She shakes her head. "This is too much, Tash."

"Look." Natasha shows her a simple purple toy. It's thick, but not crazy and it vibrates in Rhea's hand, making her shiver. "See, that's not so terrifying, is it?"

"No." Rhea admits slowly.

Natasha smiles, "There's my girl. "So, I recommend this one and ...." She looks through the shelves, "This one for you. It sucks your clit really hard, and of course you can change the setting and ... What? Why are you looking at me like that?"

"Why do you know about this?"

"Because I have one of these," She points to the vibrator, then the other one that is pink, has a circle, and a splash of water behind it on the front cover. "And this one has excellent reviews online. I've actually considered buying one myself."

"Okay then you get it."

"Will you just trust me, R?" Natasha huffs. "I'm going to get some stuff of my own but I happen to know that you have nothing to take care of yourself with."

Rhea flinches at that. She's never seen herself that way before. She's been turned on sure. Uncomfortably turned on and didn't know how to take care of it. Porn felt wrong, and she never wanted to touch herself or do anything like that. It just felt ... awkward. If no one else wanted to touch her, she'd just wait until she found someone who did.

"We've shared the same room for four years and I haven't once heard you masturbate."

"I don't think that's the point of having a roommate." Rhea hisses back.

"I'm just saying, it will do you good. My brain always feels more open after a good session. And what's the worst that can happen if you try?"

"I'm scarred for life." Rhea sets the sucking toy back, not even wanting to deal with that. "This isn't my kind of thing, Tash. And you keep talking about some bet."

"It was a pact, a deal. We agreed if we were still virgins at the end of this semester, we'd take care of that with each other."

"That was a joke." Rhea insists again.

"Nope, we're not leaving out into the real world, the mean cruel world, without taking care of that little detail of our life first." Natasha continues looking through things. She holds up a box that shows a girl wearing a dildo like it's her own cock. "What do you think?"

"That I can't take any of this seriously," Rhea said staring at the box in Natasha's hand.

"I'm buying it, you into anything else? Maybe being tied up, spanked?"

Rhea's face burns with embarrassment. "I will buy this toy if you do not ask another question in public."

"Deal,"

Rhea tries to keep her face down as she walks through the aisles, but her eyes catch on nipple clamps which happen to be right next to butt plugs. She knows what they are since she's not living under a rock and Natasha doesn't hesitate to tell her everything she doesn't want to know about the porn Natasha watches.

And she's been curious about those two specifically. She bites her lip, but makes sure not to stop walking forward. One toy, in and out (no pun intended) then back to studying like she wanted to be doing this whole time.

Numbers and make since which is why she's going to graduate as a poly-sci and math major. Eager to work in DC and change the way the nation deals with and addresses homelessness.

With numbers and policies on her side, she'll be unstoppable.

"Is this all, ma'am?" The very bored guy at the counter asks before actually looking at her. He smiles at her and looks over the toy. "I think this is a good model, but it's not for beginners."

He pulls it out, puts batteries in it and sets it in her palm as he slowly increases the speed. His gaze is hot as he watches Rhea's reaction. "Like it?"

"Um, Yeah. It's ... strong." Rhea swallows, trying to push down her blush and shake her tongue loose.

"Well, it's one of our best sellers." He finishes ringing her up and winks at her. "Let me know if you have any questions about usage, cleaning, or if you have any problems satisfying with that."

Rhea shakes her head and leaves the store as quickly as possible, hearing Natasha's hoarse laughter behind her. Natasha can be such a bitch sometimes. So pushy and demanding, sure, it can help things get done and it's why she's going to have no problem in the physical therapy world, but it can be frustrating.

When Natasha comes out, Rhea shakes her head. "What was all that about?"

"You mean the cashier definitely wanting to get into your shorts?" Natasha whacks Rhea with a flogger she bought. The sharp sting on the back of Rhea's thighs makes that familiar wetness pool low in her stomach. "If you don't want me, why don't you try him on? He was practically drooling over you."

"Don't tease me."

She holds her hands up. "I'm not. I bet he left his phone number in your bag. Did you really not catch the flirting, the way he was eying you hungrily, all that? I bet if you called him tonight, he'd come all the way over from wherever he lives and take care of that pesky virginity."

Rhea shakes her head. "No. I won't just jump into bed with a stranger, especially not for my first time."

Natasha wraps her arm around Rhea's shoulders. "I hear that. Apparently, we're both stuck looking for someone we know and trust. Good thing we have each other."

CHAPTER 3

Natasha shows Rhea all the things she bought, a flogger, the nipple clamps that Rhea lingered at, a medium sized butt plug, the clit sucking toy, and the strap on. Rhea's face goes scarlet and Natasha shakes her head.

"Don't worry, babe, only half of it is for you – and it's a hell of a maybe, okay? I wanted this toy." She points to the clit sucking toy. "And I'm curious about some of this other stuff. I figure why I should hold onto the money I've worked so hard for and not enjoy it when I have more schooling to deal with in the near future."

"I can't believe this is our last summer together." Rhea sighs, sitting on the couch in their apartment.

Natasha doesn't like thinking about it honestly. A part of her, a huge part, is going to Miss Rhea ... she hasn't even prepared to leave her best friend. She's not sure she can. Is there any preparation that can make it less painful when you have to say goodbye?

She shakes her head of that that thought. "The last week of summer we're allowed to be sad, not until then, okay?"

"Another deal?"

"Well, we're just so good at them." Natasha sticks her tongue out. "Have you even kissed someone?"

Rhea glares at her. "I have."

"Made out," Natasha leans towards Rhea, bracing her hands on her best friend's thighs when Rhea sits down. "Gone the bases?"

"What bases?"

Natasha sits on Rhea's lap and teases the low collar of her shirt. "First base is kissing. Second base is having your boobs felt – under the shirt – third base is being naked, with some implied fingering, and fourth base is sex."

She rolls her eyes. She's known the bases since middle school when her mom played that one Meatloaf song and her dad yelled at her for signing along when she'd just thought it was about playing games.

Her mom had explained, Natasha had been thoroughly grossed out, and then avoided guys for years worried that any of them that knew about baseball or the bases would try to stick their hands up her shirt.

But now, sitting on Rhea's lap, watching her eyes get all big and her chest heat up pink, Natasha wanted to be the one rounding the bases. "Want to try?"

"Tash ..."

"Unless you have a guy you want to screw before the end of the week, in which case, I'll keep my hands to myself."

Rhea bites her bottom lip. "I haven't even gone to third base on myself."

Natasha blinks a few times. "Hold up. You've never made yourself come?"

"Well, in high school, I wore shorts on the bus one day, and I found that if the seam rubbed a certain spot, it felt really good so I got kind of excited over that, but I stopped when I saw some other kid watching me."

"Okay, well it's like that, only you get to have fireworks at the end because I swear, that's what a good orgasm feels like."

"I feel like you shouldn't know all that." Rhea grumbles.

"Do you trust me, R?"

Despite her nervous eyes, she nods slowly. "Because I'm clearly an idiot, I do."

Natasha leans forward and slowly cups Rhea's face in her hands. Rhea's always been beautiful and honestly, Tash can admit she's always been a little curious what R would taste like. She kisses her softly, then licks across the seam of Rhea's lips, licking deeper until her best friend opened up to her.

Rhea's nervous little breath sounds like a whimper, but Natasha kisses her again, tongue teasing deeper until Rhea moans and tugs on Natasha's shirt. Tash nods into the kiss, sucking Rhea's tongue, teasing her with soft strokes and flicks, nibbling her bottom lip.

When she finally draws back, she's wet, her blood rushing through her body along with electricity sizzling her nerves as she looks at her best friend. Rhea's blue eyes are darker and when she sucks her bottom lip between her teeth, Natasha actually moans.

"You taste even better than I thought you would."

"You've thought about it?"

Natasha nods, stroking along the neckline of Rhea's shirt. "I have. I've thought about you a lot, actually, Rhea. I never wanted to say anything because I didn't ... I thought it was because I wasn't getting laid, but I've thought about you a lot when it comes to this."

Rhea fans her face lightly and Natasha runs her fingers through Rhea's hair. "If you don't want to go through with this, it's okay. I understand and I'm not going to force you. You know that."

"I know." Rhea echoes, and then rubs Natasha's side. "But we made an agreement and ... and you're right."

"I'm right?"

"We shouldn't leave college without getting all the knowledge we can." Rhea's lips turn up slowly.

Natasha groans and kisses her again, hungrier, more demanding as her hips roll on Rhea's thighs. She's trying for slow, wants so badly to move at her best friend's pace, but it's so hard when everything in her is begging for more.

Tash slowly strokes down to Rhea's chest and cups her breasts through her shirt. Her best friend moans and slides her hands over Natasha's ass, guiding her hips as they grind on each other. Natasha knows her panties are already soaked. With all these toys laid out and every opportunity to take advantage, she knows they're going to have a wonderful summer.

CHAPTER 4

Rhea feels the tie around her neck loosen, then Natasha lifts her shirt, tossing it to the side. At first, she wants to cover her breasts and hide, but Natasha actually groans. "You're so beautiful, R. You have no idea what a knock out you are."

Swallow, Rhea lets Natasha cup her breasts and circle her hard nipples. She's always worried that they're too big, like so big that they're a joke instead of sexy, but Natasha palms them and watches with hungry eyes.

Sliding between Rhea's legs, Natasha licks over her nipple, dragging a soft pant from Rhea's throat. When Natasha's eyes meet hers, there's fire there. Natasha licks and sucks slowly, her wet tongue sliding around Rhea's hard peek.

Her legs shake and she feels that wetness that occasionally bothers her back in full force. But there's something else, a heat tearing through her as if she's going to spontaneously combust. Natasha moans and Rhea can actually feel it through her body, threatening to consume her just as Natasha switches to her other breast.

After a moment, Natasha pushes Rhea down on the couch and licks over her throat, along her collar bone and back to her breasts, squeezing them, licking them, sucking her nipples. She keeps up with the teasing until Rhea can hardly stand it.

"I bet that cashier would kill me to be right here. He'd love listening to your moans, love being the one to kiss you and touch you." Natasha purrs, running her hand down Rhea's belly, the heat following every stroke of her fingers. "Do you want more?"

Rhea bites her lip, not sure. Natasha kisses her belly. "I won't give you more until you ask for it, R."

"Please." It comes out before she can stop it, like she has no control over her tongue. "Don't stop, Tash."

"Good girl."

The warmth in those two words make Rhea feel higher and better than any bit of praise or positive test feedback she's ever gotten. She groans as Natasha drags her shorts and panties down, kissing along her hip.

"You're so wet already." Natasha pants. "Just like me."

"That's not a bad thing?"

Natasha shakes her head and returns her attention to Rhea's breasts as her finger slides between Rhea's thighs, brushing her clit as both girls' groan. "No. It's good, very good."

Rhea's lip's part and she gasps as Natasha keeps circling that pleasurable little button between her legs. Her hips move to meet Natasha's hand and her best friend grins before pushing two fingers inside her.

Rhea's hips buck up as her eyes roll back. She pants and grabs at the couch as Natasha fingers her deep. Natasha pants. "You're so tight too. I can't believe you've never fingered yourself, R. You're a treat. You feel so good."

"I …" Rhea can't even make a sentence form. She pants and tries to hold out, but Natasha knows just what she's doing. Her fingers work deeper, filling Rhea up in a way she's never felt. When she feels like she's about to fall into oblivion, pleasure crashes through her like lightning, arching her back as moans tear from her throat.

She comes down from the high and finds Natasha stripping herself. Rhea looks her over slowly, taking in her small, perky breasts, her flat belly, and her shaved pussy and licks her lips. Natasha strokes over her body, rubbing her nipples with the wet fingers that were just buried inside Rhea.

"Do you want to touch me, Rhea?" Natasha asks.

Rhea nods hopelessly. Natasha grins. "Then you're going to taste yourself on my nipples and slide your fingers inside me. If you do that, maybe I'll let you taste me."

"I don't know how."

"I'm more than happy to teach you."

Rhea obeys as Natasha pulls her up and climbs on her lap. Rhea uses her tongue over Natasha's hard nipples just likes she did only moments ago, tasting her own salty-sweetness on Natasha. Her best friend groans and fists Rhea's hair, pulling her where she wants her to go.

"Now your fingers, inside me," Natasha pants.

Again, Rhea obeys, stroking between Natasha's legs until she moans. Rhea exploits that spot, the little nub that makes Natasha pant and groan. Natasha groans. "Inside, I said."

Rhea pushes two fingers in and obeys Natasha's slow commands, how to stroke, where to focus, to do more than just stick her fingers in and pull them out. Natasha pants and rides Rhea's fingers while Rhea kisses across her chest and throat, devouring every bit of her that she can.

Just before Natasha can come, she pushes Rhea back again. "You're going to make me come with your mouth."

Rhea swallows, unsure how to do that, unsure what that even means, but she nods, hopelessly turned on by the sounds pouring out of Natasha's mouth. She'd do anything to keep this going.

Natasha climbs up Rhea's body until she straddles Rhea's face. Her fingers spread her pussy, showing how pink and wet she is. Rhea swallows, and then licks from the entrance to the clit and back. Natasha moans and nods, grabbing something as Rhea does it again, savoring how Tash tastes and then focusing on her clit.

Natasha continues giving directions, telling her when to suck, when to lick, where to focus, then a buzzing fills the air. Rhea looks up at Natasha. She holds the purple vibrator that Rhea bought.

It comes down between Rhea's legs and rubs right against her clit, making her pant and moan as she feasts on Natasha's pussy. Natasha nods. "Keep going. Make me come, be my good girl, and I'll fuck you with this."

Rhea obeys, licking hungrily, her arms wrapped around Natasha's thighs as the vibrations from the toy pulse through her. The closer she gets Natasha the closer Rhea gets to the edge. Just when she's sure she's going to go insane, Natasha comes, slick and loud and Rhea answers with an orgasm of her own.

Natasha rolls off and they lay together on the couch, sweating, panting, and exhausted. Natasha flicks off the vibrator. "I think the rest is going to have to wait for later. Let's get a shower and I'll teach you how to masturbate."

"That doesn't sound like a break."

Natasha grins and kisses Rhea slowly. "You'll love it."

CHAPTER 5

As finals continue the girls take more than one study break. Natasha shows Rhea videos of scissoring and they try that, but Natasha doesn't think it feels as good as being eaten out. That was definitely amazing. They masturbate together while watching porn and kiss each other, always coming back together.

Rhea's still shy about it, and tries to turn everything back to finals. But once those are done, the big question still remains, "Rhea, it's the last day of exams and we're still technically virgins."

"No way, we've done ... stuff."

"We've done oral and fingering and scissoring. But if a guy asks if you're a virgin, you still technically are." Natasha says, then pulls out the strap on, which is thinner and the vibrating toy that Rhea bought which is definitely thicker. "Today we're going to fix that."

Rhea chews her bottom lip. "Is it going to hurt?"

"For a second," Natasha nods. She's taken a bigger toy, one that she's kept secret from even Rhea. "But then it just feels good. I promise."

Rhea bites her lip. "You haven't led me the wrong way yet." She sighs, giving in. "But let's start with the thin one?"

"You got it."

After plenty of kissing, licking, touching, and teasing, Natasha gets Rhea on her hands and knees. She uses the vibrator across Rhea's clit, making her pant and shake, and then Natasha puts on the strap on. She's never used one, but if a guy can figure out how to use his cock, she can figure this out right?

She kisses the back of Rhea's shoulder. "Are you ready, gorgeous?"

"Yes. Yes." Rhea chants, her hands curling into their rug. "Please, Natasha. Fuck me."

"Such a good girl," Natasha groans, giving her a slow, shallow thrust. Rhea moans and drops to her elbows. Natasha can't wait to use the flogger and maybe the anal plug too. She strokes in again, deeper this time and Rhea shivers and hisses between her lips. It's thicker here and Natasha knows to take her time. "How are you feeling, check in with me."

"It's good ... but a lot."

"That's why we started with this one, sweetheart." Natasha reminds, thrusting again.

There's a little buzzing across her clit as the toy moves and brushes that area. Once Rhea gives a nearly strangled groan, so overwhelmingly pleased, Natasha takes it up a notch, fucking her hard and fast, watching her Rhea's ass bounce against her as she takes it over and over again.

Natasha can't resist the temptation to tease Rhea's asshole with her thumb after sucking it. Rhea moans and looks back, nodding. "Please?"

"Oh, you want me to touch you right here?" Natasha puts more pressure on Rhea's ass while fucking her harder. "You want me to own all your holes?"

"Fuck." Rhea groans.

Natasha knows it's dirtier than anything she's ever said to her best friend, but Rhea's hazy eyes, the way her cheeks flush, how wet she is, it's driving Natasha insane. Rhea nods. "Yes. Please. Yes."

Natasha grins and pushes her thumb into Rhea's ass. All at once she comes, hard and fast, gushing over the strap on and shivering before nearly collapsing. Natasha rubs her ass while freeing her finger.

"What a good girl. You came so hard for me. Did that feel good?"

"Yes." Rhea pants. "So good,"

"Now we're going to go up to this." Natasha moves the vibrator to Rhea's entrance. "You're all nice and wet, so excited, I know you can take it."

"Really!" Rhea asks. "Are you sure?"

"I'll make sure you feel good. You keep this up and by the end of summer I'll be able to fuck you with a butt plug in your ass and nipple clamps hanging from your tits."

That seems to do the trick. Rhea groans and gives in. It takes more work this time. She's so tight, even with Natasha's clit sucking toy exactly where it needs to be and moans pouring from Rhea's throat, its' a tight squeeze.

One Natasha is able to work the thicker vibrator in, Rhea comes immediately. But Natasha doesn't stop. There's something about making Rhea come apart that makes Natasha even more turned on, knowing that it's because of her that her best friend can't control herself, that it's Natasha giving all this pleasure.

Once she comes again, Natasha undoes her strap on, then turns off the vibrating toy. Rhea quickly turns off the sucking toy. She looks at Natasha with that warm haze still over her eyes. "I need to make you come."

"Yes, you do, good girl. Come use that sweet tongue on me and finger me until I come for you."

Rhea smiles and gets down on her knees as Natasha sits on the couch. Rhea licks up Natasha's thighs, behaving like the good submissive she is. When she takes too long, Natasha grabs the flogger and flicks it over Rhea's round ass.

Rhea yips, but doesn't move any faster. Natasha groans and flicks her wrist two more times, hearing the swat of the leather tendrils across Rhea's body. "I want your mouth on my pussy now!"

Instantly, Rhea obeys licking and sucking as her fingers work deep. Natasha rolls her hips against Rhea's mouth, taking what she needs while Rhea moans and whispers how good Natasha tastes.

This summer is starting to look very bright indeed.

CHAPTER 6

Natasha lays with Rhea, stroking her sides. She can't believe how fast summer has passed. They're staring at the "one week" next mark and neither of them has talked about it. Rhea swallows it back. Any time it gets brought up it leads to sex. It's always hot and just like Natasha hinted they've been trying more and more things, alone and together.

Rhea can't believe she went so long without touching herself, without allowing herself to be close to another person, but now come the labels. When they leave are they going to go find boyfriends? Their friendship will continue and maybe they'll share some dirty videos, but what comes next?

Natasha swats Rhea's ass. "Are you in the mood?"

"I'm in *a* mood."

Natasha lifts Rhea's chin and studies her face before nodding. She hugs her tightly. "I'm going to miss you. I don't know what we're going to do after four years together."

Rhea sniffles and nods. "I don't know. I ... I like you a lot, Tash. I like what we have."

"I do too, but we knew it was temporary."

"I think we were only supposed to do it once." Rhea sighs, thinking of when they went out and bought the double dildo which made scissoring a lot more fun, explosively fun. And they'd gone all summer without fighting, a true miracle.

"Once is impossible with you." Natasha sighs. "Whoever gets you is going to be the luckiest person alive."

"I want to try the anal plug." Rhea decides after a while. She knows it's likely to hurt and push all her limits, but what's the harm in trying? Natasha has made everything else feel so sinfully, beautifully good.

"Are you sure?"

"You're good at keeping control and knowing my limits." Rhea agrees. "I trust you."

Natasha swallows and nods. They make out, licking and kissing slowly as heat courses through Rhea's body, igniting a hunger that she's learned to expect with Natasha. Natasha teases her with her fingers, stroking her clit without giving anything else.

They end up in her bed, and Natasha attaches the nipple clamps slowly, licking, and teasing Rhea's nipples before the pinch of pain spread across Rhea's chest, making her even wetter. She doesn't understand why pain seems to magnify every single bit of pleasure, but it does and she stopped questioning it quickly.

"Roll over for me, gorgeous." Natasha whispers.

Obediently, Rhea gets on her hands and knees. Natasha uses the vibrator on her, teasing her clit until Rhea's on the edge of coming. Right before Natasha thrusts into Rhea's pussy with the double dildo that's definitely buried in Natasha's pussy, Rhea feels something wet spread over her asshole.

"This will make it feel even better." Natasha promises, kissing over her back as the dildo teases Rhea's entrance. "I don't want you in pain."

Rhea moans and nods. Natasha ups the speed of the vibrator and thrusts into Rhea's pussy slowly, working her with teases that only make her more aware of what's to come, when Natasha finally starts pushing the plug in, Rhea pants.

"Relax." Natasha croons, rubbing the vibrator over Rhea's clit until she does. Her body swallows up the anal plug, weighing Rhea down with pleasure and filling her up twice as much as she's used to.

She knows she won't last long, not with all this going on, her nipples being tugged with each move by the clamps, her ass all full and stretched, the vibrator buzzing across her clit again and again and Natasha fucking her.

"You have no idea how sexy this is how hot you are." Natasha groans, thrusting again.

"You turn me on so much." Another thrusts and Natasha moans. "Fuck you're so tight, I feel the dildo moving in me."

Rhea whimpers, then all out groans when Natasha plays with the anal plug, grinding it harder into her body, then tugging gently, never all the way out, but just enough for that friction to sweep through and ruin any of Rhea's sanity.

They fuck hard and fast, the only way Natasha does, their pussies brushing as they take the double dildo together, over and over, moans and wet sounds filling the room while Rhea tries to cling to anything she can possibly grab onto.

But it's too much. Every thrust makes the nipple clamp tug and the vibrations and anal plug moving are just too intense with Natasha fucking her. Rhea bites her lip. "Please let me come! Oh fuck, let me come. Please!"

"I love when you beg. Come for me, sexy girl."

Rhea explodes, drenching the dildo as her body tightens around the plug. The orgasm drags on as Natasha keeps fucking her and the chain between her nipples weighs down. Finally, Natasha comes too, panting and moaning.

Rhea stays still as Natasha takes care of all their toys, one at a time, then they get in the shower together. Natasha helps Rhea to stand for a while, and then they give up and just sit in the tub, wrapped around each other.

Rhea lifts her head to look at Natasha despite the haze over her eyes. "I'm going to miss you so much."

"You're going to miss the good sex." Natasha rolls her eyes.

Rhea shakes her head. "You're my best friend, Tash. I love you. This just … it's brought us closer. I really don't know what I'm going to do without you one room over."

Natasha's eyes water and she looks away. "None of that, if you cry, I'll cry, and then we'll both be crying messes."

"I'm sorry." Rhea hugs her tightly and lets out a few tears. "This is so hard."

"That's what she said."

"Oh, shut up." Rhea laughs and shakes her head.

They get out of the shower, get dressed, and then Natasha pulls out some vodka that came from her family in Russia. She pours them each a shot and raises her glass. "To the best summer I never expected."

Rhea clinks and they both take a shot. Natasha stares at her glass, refills it and refills Rhea's. "To the only person I don't want to leave and the best friend I've ever had."

"You're going to make me cry." Rhea swallows.

"Drink!"

They both toss back the shots, and then hug each other. Rhea asks if Natasha wants her to please her, but instead they settle on ice cream and the first movie they ever watched together, cuddled up, refusing to talk about what the future might hold.

Lesbian Virgin Friend Seduction 2

Erotic Short Story
Sexy Frist Time Forbidden Hot Steamy FFF Experience

Adult Romance Fiction
LISA LICKITTY

Kindle Edition
Copyright 2021 Khelan Publishing
Published by Khelan Publishing
License Notes: This ebook is licensed for your personal enjoyment only. This ebook may not be re-sold or given away to other people. If you would like to share this ebook with another person, please purchase an additional copy for each person you share it with. If you're reading this book and did not purchase it, or it was not purchased for your use only, then you should return and purchase your own copy. Thank you for respecting the hard work of this author.
Khelan Publishing Printing March 2021
5 4 3 2 1

5 LESBIAN STEAMY FF EXPLICIT SEXY SHORT EROTIC STORIES

~

All characters in this book have no existence outside the imagination of the author and have no relation whatsoever to anyone bearing the same name or names. They are not even distantly inspired by any individual known or unknown to the author, and all incidents are pure inventions of fiction.

Table of Content

Virgin Lesbian Friend Seduction 2

    CHAPTER 1
    CHAPTER 2
    CHAPTER 3
    CHAPTER 4

CHAPTER 1

Rhea thinks about what life has been since she left college six years ago. After that last amazing summer with Natasha, they went their separate ways. They never really talked about it before Rhea headed out. She was sure that if they had a long goodbye, they'd both end up crying and maybe their future would be different, but …

Natasha went back to the small town we're from, found her high school crush, got married, had a baby, and got settled. It was never the life that Rhea wanted. Rhea went to a big city medical school to get her degree and met a woman that swept her away, from girlfriend to wife within five years.

Then, Rhea and Katie moved back home. All of one week ago after a long conversation following Rhea's mother inviting her back to fill the pediatrician position that had opened up when Old Mr. Taylor has decided retirement was necessary.

Rhea smiles at Katie as the redhead glares at the lingering boxes. Katie grumbles about a box and Rhea wraps her arms around her, kissing her neck, "Your house your rules, babe."

"And a million boxes to open!" She shakes her head. "Lucky for you I don't start at the lab for another week."

"Lucky for me you came with me." Rhea kisses her again.

It had been a big move Katie had been working for the Red Cross directly, taking blood, and running tests, putting her phlebotomy license to work in overtime. Now that would be Katie's job.

"I love you." Katie says with a grin. "Now hurry up before you're late for work. Stop stalling."

Rhea sucks her bottom lip between her teeth and Katie kisses her forehead. "You're going to knock them dead and you know it, sweetheart. The kids will love you. Even Dr. Taylor said that they're going to like you more than him."

"Well, he's half blind and doesn't know what he's talking about." She argues before stroking through Katie's thick red hair. "I'll be home for dinner."

"The best perk in the world and my favorite part of small-town living."

"Don't get too excited about that. I'm basically on call constantly."

Katie swats Rhea's butt as she heads out and both laugh. Rhea was sure that after Natasha, she'd end up heart broken and pinging for her best friend. Instead, they haven't spoken for the last five years. They managed to keep talking for the first 'after college' year. But once they ran out of things in common, were working different schedules, and Natasha went crazy with mom mode, their conversations dwindled.

Now they barely exchange happy birthday messages on Facebook. Still, being back here, Rhea can't help but look over her shoulder a few times, check any dark-haired woman walking up and down the street. When she gets to the office, she opens it up, says hi to the nurses that have more patients lined up for the day and then Rhea gets to work, blocking everything else out.

The work is pretty easy. There are physicals for school, a few colds, a sprained ankle, an allergy test, vaccines, and a boy that got over-excited when he saw some bees and grabbed one, nothing life or death so far. No wayward stray bullets. None of the intense trauma that she saw while in the city and had to prepare for accordingly.

By the end of their second week, Rhea actually feels like she's been doing this for years. All her knowledge has just been sitting there waiting for use and those few customer service jobs she worked when she could be definitely paying off.

She can wear a smile even when moms fight vaccines she gives them paperwork, goes over things, and moves on. When parents hover over her, watching her and grumbling, she just smiles at the child, winks, shares little secrets, and distracts them from whatever pain they would be feeling.

Then she sets them free.

On Friday, she gets a call from one of the nurses, Elaine, to hurry up and come in. Katie sighs and shakes her head, paint speckling her face and shirt. "Of course, you get out of house painting."

"I'll be right back. I promise." Rhea kisses her hungrily, "Because I'm excited for the cleanup."

Katie giggles and Rhea heads to the clinic.

She heads in and Elaine jumps up. "The child is haven't a reaction to something he's eaten. Based on what I saw, it doesn't look like anaphylaxis, but he's swelling up. Probably just needs Benadryl and maybe a steroid shot, but you have to sign off on everything like that."

Rhea nods and walks into the patient's room with her clip board. "So, Harvey isn't feeling great?"

"Itchy!" A boy yells, "Itchy and fat."

"Harvey, don't yell in an office."

That familiar voice gets Rhea's attention. She looks up from the clipboard and sees Natasha. Natasha looks from her son to Rhea, then her eyes widen. Natasha's thick black hair is back in a bun, there's no makeup on her face, but she looks fresh, alive, and beautiful as she always has.

The dark-haired little boy on the table makes a frustrated sound and Rhea makes herself focus on him. His cheeks are swollen, his eyes are nearly shut, but he keeps rubbing at them.

"Do you know what he ate?"

"Harvey, tell her."

"I grabbed some of Daddy's peanuts from the bar, cause I'm big." He states clearly.

"Is this the first time he's had issues with peanuts?"

"Yes! Peanut butter was his favorite thing until he decided he didn't want to eat it anymore about a year ago. It was easier just to go with it on that. Now I see why." Natasha runs her fingers through his hair. "Please help."

Rhea gives liquid Benadryl – blue berry flavor – and Harvey asks for more. She shakes her head, but gives him a steroid as well to bring down the swelling more quickly. Rhea offers to let them stay until they notice a clear improvement in Natasha's son, and then walks out of the office, trying to catch her breath.

CHAPTER 2

Natasha keeps stroking Harvey's hair back and away from his face. He yawns and complains about being tired. She encourages him to sleep while trying to think if she'd heard that Rhea was back in town. Last she knew, she was studying at some fancy medical school two states over.

"Mommy, I like the new doctor. She has good flavors."

Natasha smiles at such an innocent comment. Especially since she remembers how Rhea tastes. "You like her?"

"Yes. Dr. Thomas is nice." He nods, as if confirming the most important thing.

Natasha smiles, "I'm going to go talk to the doctor, okay."

"Imma sleep."

"I bet you are. Take all the sleep you need. We'll build a blanket fort when we get home and Daddy will join us." She promises.

When Harvey's eyes shut and stay shut for more than a moment, she slips out the door and sees Rhea, wearing reading glasses, filling out forms. "I didn't know you were here."

"Would you have come if you did?" Rhea asks.

Natasha remembers that painful morning she woke up and found a note from Rhea. She understood it. Saying goodbye after their summer together would have been too hard and Rhea was right. There's no way they would have moved on. Natasha would have pulled her close, begged her to try long distance and knowing both of them, they would have ended up fighting nearly constantly.

"Yes." Natasha whispers.

Rhea sighs and turns to face her, "Really? Because our last full conversation ..."

"I was drunk and frustrated." She admits. "I mean, I felt like I lost my best friend. You were supposed to come visit that summer and just didn't. And you'd already cancelled our Christmas plans. I felt like I didn't have a place in your life anymore and that hurt."

Rhea rubs her forehead. "I was nervous. I had a girlfriend; you were seeing Justin. I just ... I figured that was the end of our friendship after everything. I didn't want it to be. Between the stress of school and seeing how excited you were to be pregnant; I just didn't think we had anything in common anymore."

Natasha nods. That's a fair point. Their lives had moved in completely different directions. After college, Natasha had come home and worked a string of jobs, finding out quickly that a bachelor's degree didn't guarantee everything.

Then she'd reconnected with Justin and life had been a whirlwind. They'd had an epic love story, warm, amazing, and then Harvey. Justin's a great dad, but all the passion in their life is gone. He's tired constantly and Harvey just doesn't know that he's faking it.

Natasha bites her bottom lip and rubs the back of her head. "Well, we should get dinner and catch up."

"Dinner's possible."

"Lunch is probably better though, Justin's off on Saturday. I am sure he'll be able to watch Harvey during the day. Are you off?"

"Unless someone has an allergic reaction or emergency," Rhea teases.

Natasha smiles, then they get Harvey. He looks so much better and it's only been fifteen minutes. The swelling has gone down and he's sleeping peacefully. Natasha lifts him into her arms, offers to pay, but Rhea lets her know there's an online portal now so she can do that later.

She leaves with one last look back at Rhea.

What would their lives be like if one of them had just pushed for the relationship? Natasha had thought about it. She can admit that as she buckles her son into his car seat. There's been more than one occasion where she wishes she would have just shown up at Rhea's school.

Anytime she's fought with Justin over the years, it's been Rhea on her mind. Even once Harvey was born, she's wondered if Rhea ever wanted kids, if there was ever a chance. But now that she knows Rhea's taken, it's an even hazier picture.

Natasha shakes her head. They'll have lunch, catch up, find out exactly how different their lives are and then she'll be able to move on happily. That's the whole point, right? Natasha takes a deep breath and tries not to remember the kinky post-college summer they shared. All the things they tried, what Rhea looks like when she comes, and how it feels to hold her close, every smile and laugh they shared

It's the past. They're lucky to have the time they did and Natasha can't quite shake the feeling that they're done and she'll only have those memories to mock her whenever she looks at Justin, watches him drink three beers in a row, and his gut come in more. She'll think about what she could have had with Rhea, the life built on love, connection, friendship, instead of dating and an oops that led to marriage and a baby.

"Mommy," Harvey said as she picks him up and carries him inside. "Dr. Thomas is pretty."

"Yes, she is."

"I like her candy." He wraps his arms around Natasha's neck and her chest fills with love.

No matter how life could have been, she loves Harvey. She loves being a mom and loves feeling so complete and happy by spending every day with him. When she comes inside, Justin looks at Harvey, then her.

"Is he okay?"

"Yeah, His throat didn't close. We just have to be careful with peanuts now."

"Yes, Mommy, I didn't like it. Tasted like ... itchy." Harvey hums.

Justin laughs and takes him, bouncing Harvey on his hip. "Good thing you have such a smart mom." Justin kisses her cheek, always her cheek now, and takes Harvey to bed. "Let's go cuddle."

"Okay, Daddy ... can we have dinner later?"

Natasha smiles, but rubs her arms. Without Harvey close, the loneliness seeps in and she can't wait for Saturday to come around.

CHAPTER 3

Rhea gets herself ready, pulling on a cute top and jeans. Katie's working on her business in the bedroom. Rhea peeks out of the bathroom. "How's the novel going, babe?"

"This one is better than the last few from this writer. Still requires some rewrites and edits, but there's a plot."

"And the characters?"

"Actually likeable," Katie looks up, her hair in a messy bun, a hickey on her neck and looks over Rhea. "You look cute."

"Thanks. I'm meeting with that friend from college I told you about on Wednesday."

"The one who opened your eyes to the lesbian side of things?" Katie teases before motioning Rhea over. "Remind me to thank her."

They share a toe-curling kiss and Rhea can't deny that despite all the ways life could have gone, she loves Katie. She's bright and sweet. She's sarcastic at times, but her humor and drive bring a newness to life that Rhea can't ignore.

She sighs and rubs Katie's cheek. "I love you so much. I can't imagine not having you in my life."

"Well, I certainly appreciate that, considering we kind of went and did the marriage thing so now you're stuck with me."

"Blessed with you, Katie."

"Yes, Doctor." She giggles.

Rhea heads out, meeting Natasha at the little bistro she talked about when she was in the doctor's office. After a deep breath, she heads in. Natasha jumps up and beams. "You came."

"We made a promise, I kept it," Rhea smiles. "And I have plenty to hear about, I'm sure."

"Me too," Then to the hostess came, "Is there anything available on the patio? It's such a beautiful day." Rhea asked.

They head there and Natasha orders a mimosa. She shakes her head. "I never drink with Harvey around. He wants to try everything I have, even if he ends up hating it. I'm not allowed to eat without help."

"He's cute."

"He's not usually so loud and demanding. But because of the peanut thing, he said he was too itchy to eat dinner, even his favorite. When a kid turns down dinosaur chicken nuggets, it's time to bring them to the doctor."

"That is incredibly true." Rhea laughs. "He's so big. Five years old already?"

"Yeah!"

Natasha talks about how everything happened. She and Justin were just dating. He works at the high school as an A.P. Art History teacher and the football coach. Natasha is lucky to be a stay-at-home mom. She started a blog about being a mom and trying different activities and things that are recommended online so she still has some income.

It sounds like a good life for her. Rhea's happy she has it, until she looks to the side, takes a long drink from her mimosa and a frown tug at her lips. Rhea leans her head to the side, but promises herself she's not going to push. This is a friendly meeting. She'll take everything at face value and wait to dive in.

She's sure that this won't be the last time they see each other. It's a small town and things happen here all the time. Natasha smiles "So, what about you? I haven't seen your wife around … I don't think."

"She's a home body." Rhea laughs. "She is an editor for a publishing house. She loves being home and making our house comfortable. We just finished painting yesterday and unpacked the last box."

Rhea continues, talking about how they met –Rhea thought she was going out with someone she met online, but the guy stood her up. Katie had been the bartender who listened to her and somehow, they ended up going home together, but after talking for hours after having sex, they realized it was more than a one-night stand, even if Rhea was crazy busy, Katie was always making time for them, texting her, making sure Rhea didn't get away.

"After all that chasing, I figured it was time to make it official. We've been together ever since."

Natasha beams and dabs at her eyes. "Sorry, I cry more easily now. That's amazing. I'd love to meet her."

They keep catching up and leave with the promise of seeing each other again. As the weeks continue, they meet up for occasional lunches and then Rhea finally brings Katie along. Katie wears a cute yellow dress that makes her hair look all the brighter and keeps picking at her neckline.

"Do you think it's too low? I mean ... I don't want to be your hussy or something."

"If anyone would dare say that about you, I'd set them straight fast."

"I'm just the trophy wife."

"Oh, don't get me wrong, you're definitely the hot one." Rhea kisses her cheek. "But you have more brains than anyone I've met. The house would fall apart without you."

"You guys are cute." Natasha says, joining them.

She introduces herself, smiles at them both and motions to the table. Harvey's with her and Rhea sees Katie's nervousness. They agreed early on they didn't want kids, but he's cute and sweet and has won over Katie by the end of the night. Rhea also notices the way that Katie plays with her necklace while looking at Natasha.

When their guests run to the bathroom, Katie leans towards her. "She's the one, right?"

"Yes." Rhea blushes.

Katie nods. "Maybe we should see if she's still interested in women. It's been a while since we've had a third."

"Naughty." Rhea giggles, then rubs over the inside of Katie's knee. "I'll start dropping hints when her child isn't nearby. But she's married, so we can't expect much."

"I have a feeling she'll jump on the opportunity." Katie assures, kissing Rhea softly. "And if not, it just means I get you all to myself."

Rhea nods. She takes Natasha out few more times before Natasha agrees to come over to see the house and have dinner. She says Justin will come, but at the last minute he cancels so Natasha comes over alone.

Katie smirks at Rhea. "How have those hints been going?"

"I guess we'll find out tonight."

CHAPTER 4

Natasha comes into the house and looks around at all the art, the framed pieces, the décor that's so different from what Rhea had up in their room. Rhea hugs her and Natasha sighs as she feels Rhea's curves press to hers. It's so familiar, she's familiar, warm, and Natasha can't help but remember what it was like to be together during that summer.

Katie joins them with an apron on. She looks cute, like a fifty's housewife, minus the giant poufy dress. Katie grins and hugs Natasha. "Sorry, I'm a hugger."

"I don't mind."

And she doesn't. Lately, she's noticed the way Rhea looks at her when they meet up, she's caught those little hints and comments, but she wasn't sure they were serious. Rhea's always been flirtatious, but it's felt like a test and even though she and her husband have an understanding where Natasha is allowed to be with women once in a while as long as Justin doesn't know and there's not a man involved, restarting with Rhea feels dangerous.

"It's good to see you both." Natasha says.

"And you! You look good." Katie compliments. "Better than dinner even."

Rhea shoves her playfully and Katie kisses Rhea's neck. "And you're down right edible."

Natasha feels a pang of jealousy for that. The easy compliments the loving looks, the undercurrent of attraction. Rhea takes Natasha's hand. "Come on. Dinner is just about ready."

"It smells great." Natasha says. "You have such a lovely house."

"Thank you. Katie has a good eye for décor. I swear, she can find everything valuable at thrift shops."

Dinner goes easily, but the comments keep adding up. When Katie serves dessert, she takes Rhea's hand. All the flirting, the biting-lip glances that Natasha has gotten, the soft touches, lingering looks, it has Natasha on edge and ready to go. She actually feels wet, which is amazing.

"So, Rhea's too shy to outright ask ..." Katie murmurs.

Natasha looks between them nervously.

"We're interested in you. Would you like to act on that?" Katie says. When Natasha doesn't answer immediately, Katie laughs. "I mean, do you want to have a threesome?"

"Um, I don't know. I'll have to think about it. I'm not sure." Natasha hedges.

She hasn't been in a threesome, ever. It's an interesting thought, but it hurts a little to think that's the only reason they've been spending time with her when she has so few friends. Rhea shrugs and rubs Natasha's hand.

"Either way, we like having you around. I was so worried people wouldn't accept us because we're ... you know."

"That's not a problem here, not anymore." Natasha assures.

But by the time she leaves, her chest feels lighter. Knowing that they want to keep seeing her either way, knowing that she's not about to lose the two friends she's made who don't eyeball her husband ... it's comforting.

Justin looks up when she comes in. "How was dinner?"

"It was good. It's nice seeing a friend from college doing so well." Natasha says, kissing his cheek. "How was your night?"

"Harvey was a ball of energy, but I finally got him down." Justin says. "Ready for bed?"

"Yeah. I just have to get through a shower." She kisses him full on the mouth, but he draws back after a moment and she sucks her bottom lip.

Justin just stares after her. It's been a long time since they'd even had sex. Natasha gets in the shower and thinks about the offer. Rhea wants her and she can't stop thinking about it. She can't help but remembering the near constant orgasms that they shared together. And adding in another person, her wife, being taken by two women being doted on with all the heat and hunger she misses ...

Natasha slides her hands over her breasts, circling her nipples as she pictures Rhea's loud moans as she comes, how wet she gets. She pictures Katie's tight body, her round ass, thick thighs, all of it bare and rubbing against her. Natasha's fingers dip between her thighs and she rubs her clit slowly, picturing Rhea on her knees, licking her pussy while Katie sucks and teases Natasha's breasts.

When her fingers push inside her wet pussy, rubbing that spot that she's learned gets her off the fastest, she comes apart, quiet as she's learned to be, and pants as she braces herself against the tile wall and swallows hard.

Just like that her mind is made up. The heat with Justin is gone. She's not sure if it left when she had the baby or even before. They live well together, they parent well together, they're comfortable, but their sex life is dry and Natasha's tired of settling for an occasional fun night once a month, if she's lucky.

When she gets dressed and lays in bed, Justin is already snoring. She pulls out her phone and texts Rhea. "I'm in. Next weekend?"

The response is nearly immediately "Can't wait!"

Now all she has to do is wait, not talk herself out of it, and not let any of the other over-gossipy housewives know what her plan is. She goes to sleep, still thinking about Katie and Rhea, not sure how she's going to last an entire week before seeing them again.

CHAPTER 5

Katie spot cleans, then looks around. Rhea laughs and pulls her close by her hips, kissing her hungrily. The week dragged by, but Katie was so focused on keeping the house presentable and getting all her work done, she's been a stressed-out mess.

"You know, I could go for a snack before we have company and you look like you're exactly what I need." Rhea teases.

Katie sighs. "I know I'm acting crazy. We haven't done this in so long. Are you sure she's up for it and doesn't just want another round with you?"

"I'm sure." Rhea promises. "We're all going to have a great time. We have our toys ready."

"The thick dildo for the strap on is right where it belongs. Then we have the thinner one. A few anal plus so she has different styles, nipple clamps, the wand. Am I missing anything?"

"The crop?" Rhea asks?

"Check."

"The ropes?"

"Ready to go."

"Then so are we." Rhea smooths down her back. Don't worry, babe. Natasha is just as excited as we are. I don't think she's ever been a sub."

"Well, we'll just make sure her pleasure is taken care of." Katie kisses Rhea again, her tongue teasing before drawing back. "And we'll all have a great time."

"You'll love how she tastes." Rhea promises. "It'll be a great night. I'm sure of it."

A knock on the door separates the two and Rhea gets it, welcoming Natasha in. She's wearing a slinky red dress that shows how perfect her body still is. Her breasts are bigger than Natasha remembers, but she's just as beautiful.

"Hey." Rhea says, shutting and locking the door.

"Hi." Natasha waves. "Are we jumping right in, having dinner?"

"We already ate, but we can play a game or we can head up to the bedroom." Katie shrugs. "It's whatever we want to do."

Natasha nods. They catch up about the week and then Natasha looks between them. "I haven't been able to stop thinking about you both. Every time I do, I end up masturbating. My shower has seen so much."

"I'd like to see that." Katie licks her bottom lip.

Rhea grins and sits beside Natasha. She twirls her finger in Natasha's thick hair. "We've been thinking about you too. About how soft your skin is." Rhea's hand glides up Natasha's arm and over her shoulder. "How intense your eyes are, all the things we'd like to do with you."

"Last time I was in control." Natasha breathes.

"And this time, you're the focus, honey." Katie says, sitting on her other side. "We want you to feel good, and maybe punish you a little."

Natasha laughs and looks between them. Katie strokes over the back of Natasha's neck, rubbing out the tension in her shoulders until she groans. Rhea leans forward and tastes the sound off her lips.

After a short pause, Natasha returns the kiss, cupping the back of Rhea's head as their tongues move together, slipping and tangling as if no time has passed at all. When Rhea draws back, she drags her fingers over the neckline of the dress before Katie guides Natasha's straps down and kisses along the back of her shoulder.

Natasha swallows as Rhea spreads her legs and strokes up her thighs. "Show us how you touch yourself, Natasha. Show us where you want us."

Natasha pulls her dress up around her hips, revealing she didn't bother to put on underwear, but did shave her pussy. Rhea licks her lips as Katie continues kissing Natasha's neck and guides the dress further down to set Natasha's breasts free.

Natasha pants as she dips a finger into her pussy and rubs her clit at the same time, her head falling onto Katie's shoulder as Katie teases her hard nipples. Rhea licks her bottom lip and readjusts, kissing along the inside of Natasha's thigh, spreading her legs wider so she can see Natasha's hand working her wet pussy.

"Oh... that feels so good." Natasha moans.

"And your pussy looks so good. So wet." Rhea locks eyes with Katie and smiles. "Delicious."

Katie grins and nibbles Natasha's neck, her fingers pinching her nipples tightly. Just before Natasha can come and before Rhea can lick across her pussy, Katie jumps up, strips Natasha, and the three head upstairs.

Natasha kisses Katie hungrily as Rhea pushes her fingers into Natasha's pussy, making both of them groan. Natasha pulls at Katie's clothes until she's just as naked, then both women turn on Rhea. Rhea licks her fingers and Katie groans, kissing her wife to taste Natasha's pussy on her lips.

Natasha licks over Rhea's nipple before sucking softly and stroking her pussy with clumsy fingers. When she pushes two in, Rhea groans. Rhea teases Natasha's pussy too, pushing her back to the bed as Katie gets all the toys they have planned to use. Katie gets her strap-on in place and ready and hands Rhea the vibrator.

Obediently, Natasha gets on the bed as she looks between the women. Rhea can feel exactly how wet and hot she is, how badly she needs this for the three of them. She ties Natasha's wrists to the bed and kisses her hungrily. "You have no idea how long we've wanted this."

"From the first time I saw you, I told Rhea we just had to." Katie agrees, rubbing the thick dildo she wears.

Natasha licks across her bottom lip. "I'm all yours."

Rhea ties her legs spread wide and nods. "Oh yes you are. And we're going to make the most of every second."

Katie climbs onto the bed and teases Natasha with the thick dildo while Rhea holds the wand to her nipples. "Ask us to stop and we'll let you go. But until then, we are going to make you come as many times as we possibly can."

Natasha moans and her body arches as Rhea moves the vibrator and Katie thrusts in deep. Katie pants. "Such a good girl already. I bet you can't wait for Rhea to take a toy to your ass too. You're such a naughty girl, I bet you want all your holes filled."

"Fuck yes." Natasha gives in.

CHAPTER 6

Natasha can't believe how easy this is or how hot. She's never taken a dildo as big as the one Katie is using to fuck her, but it feels so amazing, brushing every sensitive spot in her pussy at once. Her eyes roll back as Rhea drags the vibrator down her body, teasing her with all she can have until Rhea spreads her pussy and rubs the wand over her clit.

"Oh fuck!" Natasha shouts. How can she be so close already?

It hurts, actually hurts when Katie stops thrusting and leans forward to bite Natasha's nipple. She's not gentle at all. She licks, sucks, then bites again. Rhea does the same, licking and sucking, just to rub Natasha's nipple between her teeth.

The mix of pleasure and pain is so overwhelming, but without Katie moving and with the vibrator on such a low setting, it's torture. There's no way she's going to come. Her back arches and she pants.

"Please! More!"

Katie bites Natasha's breast, not hard enough to leave a mark, thankfully, then thrusts again. She hands something to Rhea and when Natasha's hips lift to meet the vibrator and the punishing thrust of Katie's dildo, she feels something nudge into her ass.

"Oh!"

"How's that?" Rhea asks in her ear. "You want your ass filled with this plug?"

"Yes!" Natasha pants. "Oh yes. Please."

"Take it." Katie orders, thrusting even harder.

Natasha's lips open but no sound comes out. Her eyes roll back as Rhea ups the vibrations and Natasha comes down on the anal plug. It's a tight fit, almost painful as she takes it all the way, but it feels so good. She's so full, so overwhelmed, and this is just the beginning? It's impossible.

Rhea hands the wand to Katie and Katie steals Natasha's mouth in a kiss that curls her toes and threatens to make her come right away. Her whole body is trembling, even from just the air stroking her skin.

Katie ups the wand all the way, sending so much power through Natasha's body as Katie fucks her harder, faster, that Natasha knows she can't stop herself. She tugs on the restraints, then almost screams as she comes.

Smiling, Katie kisses her again, and slides out. Natasha whimpers. "But ..."

"You're nowhere near done, honey." Katie promises.

Rhea wears a strap-on that's slightly smaller and she gets between Natasha's legs and fucks her hard. Natasha moans, but her head is turned to the side and Katie pushes her dildo into Natasha's mouth, gagging her.

Natasha moans as she tastes herself on the silicone and sucks obediently as Katie fingers herself. Natasha tries to pull at the restraints again, wanting to touch and please as much as they are, but she's not allowed. The restraints don't give.

They go over and over, switching positions again and again. Natasha loses track of how often she comes, but when she's untied and nipple clamps are put on her, she looks at the women with confusion. It only grows when the anal plug is slid from her body.

"I don't want to be done."

"You're not." Rhea says from behind her. "You're going to take us both."

Natasha moans and nods. Katie slides into her pussy as Rhea takes her ass and they fuck her in a rhythm that makes every nerve burn and sizzle. Natasha's never felt anything so intense in her life. It's overwhelming, it's beyond any kind of ecstasy she's known.

"You're so beautiful when you come." Katie says, kissing across one side of Natasha's neck.

"It's so sexy, I feel like I can get off without touching myself." Rhea agrees, kissing the other side.

When Katie tugs the nipple clamps, pain mixes with pleasure in the best way. It's a slow torture since they stop every time Natasha gets close, but when she finally comes, when she lets the bliss and heat drag her into an earth-shattering orgasm, she soaks the dildos and the bed. Rhea and Katie moan.

Rhea rubs Natasha's pussy and shows her how wet she is, then feeds her fingers to her wife. They groan and slowly ease out of Natasha's holes.

Natasha flops back, exhausted, legs twitching, so happy as she pants.

Rhea spreads her legs and licks over her clit, then sucks while fucking her with the dildo that was on her strap on. Natasha fights to keep her eyes open as she sees Katie fuck Rhea at the same time, rocking her between them until Natasha is grabbing at the sheets to try to hold off on coming again.

Rhea groans against her pussy and those vibrations alone send her over the edge, into another panting, slow burning orgasm that rips through her body. Rhea comes too, panting against Natasha's hip.

Katie tosses the strap on, then motions for Rhea to move. She climbs on top of Natasha, her pussy right over her face and slides her hand into Natasha's sweaty hair. "It's time to make me come. Eat me out."

Natasha doesn't hesitate. She laps at Katie's wet clit, savoring her spiced honey flavor, Katie moans and Natasha notices that Rhea's eating her ass from the mirror hanging on the wall. Katie grinds between them, rocking her body back and forth before she lets her own pleasure drag her down with an intense moan.

The three collapse together in bed, Natasha cuddled between them. She's sure this is a dream. She's going to wake up wet as can be and have to beg Justin for sex or pull out one of her own toys, but Katie kisses her and grins.

"Rhea was right. You taste good."

"Told you." Rhea agrees, turning Katie's head to kiss her as well.

Katie climbs over Natasha and kisses her wife hungrily. Natasha laughs and shakes her head. "Holy shit. This ... tonight. It's amazing."

Rhea cuddles against Natasha's shoulder and Katie wraps an arm under Natasha's neck. "It doesn't have to be the last time, honey. If you want more of us, we're right here."

Rhea nods and Natasha bites her lip. "I might just take you up on that."

"I hope so." Rhea winks.

Naughty Wife Lesbian Experience

First Time FFM Sex Story
Taboo Cheating Marriage Romance

Adult Erotic Swingers Fiction
KATE KAT

Kindle Edition
Copyright 2021 Khelan Publishing
Published by Khelan Publishing
License Notes: This ebook is licensed for your personal enjoyment only. This ebook may not be re-sold or given away to other people. If you would like to share this ebook with another person, please purchase an additional copy for each person you share it with. If you're reading this book and did not purchase it, or it was not purchased for your use only, then you should return and purchase your own copy. Thank you for respecting the hard work of this author.
Khelan Publishing Printing March 2021
5 4 3 2 1

5 LESBIAN STEAMY FF EXPLICIT SEXY SHORT EROTIC STORIES 91

~

All characters in this book have no existence outside the imagination of the author and have no relation whatsoever to anyone bearing the same name or names. They are not even distantly inspired by any individual known or unknown to the author, and all incidents are pure inventions of fiction.

Table of Content

Naught Wife Lesbian Experience

> CHAPTER 1
> CHAPTER 2
> CHAPTER 3
> CHAPTER 4

CHAPTER 1

"I'll be leaving now, honey," Ben said as he leaned in to place a kiss on his wife, Genia's lips. Ben had an early morning meeting he wanted to catch up with.

"Okay, don't forget the dinner this evening," Genia had added, and Ben stopped in his tracks before he faces palmed himself. He had totally forgotten about the dinner they usually have with his friend Stevie and wife Rochelle. "Stevie!"

"You forgot?" Genia asked, with arched brows.

"It's not that. I forgot today was Thursday," Ben said.

"Thank goodness I reminded you. What's it going to be? Will you join us there or you will pick me up and we go together?" Genia asked.

"If my meetings run late, I'm afraid I'll have to join you there," Ben said.

"Okay, that's fine," Genia said.

"Thanks babe. I love you," Ben said.

"I love you too," Genia said before Ben left the bedroom and the apartment. Genia sighed after he left. She wished the time for the dinner would draw closer. The reason wasn't farfetched, she wanted to see Rochelle again. Genia wondered why she was always eager to see Rochelle. She wondered if it was because they usually have a connection when they chatted. However, Genia knew better. She recalled the countless times her eyes would drift towards Rochelle's bosom. Genia knew she was endowed in the right places. She knew she could make any man lose his head with only a wink. However, she didn't know why she was always fixated with Rochelle's breast. Genia imagined what it would be like to cup Rochelle's breast through her clothes. She imagined fondling her breasts and what it would feel like to play with her nipples. Genia had average breasts and bums compared to Rochelle's.

However, the curiosity in Genia wanted to know what it would feel like to touch Rochelle's breast. Genia closed her eyes for a brief moment before she stretched to the side of the bed and opened her drawer. She grabbed her purple vibrator before she laid back on the bed. She smiled as she taught of the naughty things Ben did to her with the vibrator. She tried to push Rochelle out of her mind to focus on fantasies with Ben. She switched on the vibrator.

Genia slowly guided the vibrator to her pussy and closed her eyes. Memories of what Ben had done to her with the vibrator filled her mind. Genia let out a low moan as she rubbed the dildo over her clitoris.

"Ohh!" She loudly moaned as she twisted on the bed. She recalled how Ben had slowly guided the vibrator into her pussy and she did the same.

"Ahhh," She screamed as the sensation hit her. Genia slowly started fucking herself with the dildo. She imagined Ben rubbing her clitoris while he fucked her with the dildo. Genia let out a groan as she increased the pace of the thrust of the dildo inside herself.

Genia imagined Ben covering her nipples with his mouth.

"Yes, baby. That's it baby," Ben groaned into her ears while he continued thrusting the dildo into her.

"Yes! Yes! Yes Rochelle!" Genia screamed before she could help herself. Ben had been replaced with Rochelle in her imagination. She didn't stop to think about why she was fantasizing about her. The only thing that mattered to her at the point was to reach her climax.

"Ohhhh," Genia moaned as she rubs her clitoris with her free palm. She knew she was close to her ecstasy and was ready.

"Yes!" She screamed as an image of Rochelle covering her cunt filled her mind. What followed was Genia's ragged breathing. She was a sweating mess. Genia tried to calm her nerves as she laid on the bed. She tried to understand what she had allowed to happen again.

"What the hell is going on with me?" She muttered with a frown as she raised her palm and rested it on her forehead. Genia couldn't explain her fantasies for women. Ben was smoking hot like his friend Stevie. He had angular, jaws streaks of tattoos on his arms and toned abs.

Stevie and Ben could pass on for a woman's wet dreams. Genia satisfied all her sexual cravings had started from a teenage age. However, she knew she could get disowned back then if she acted upon it. Genia wanted to know how it felt like to be with a woman. Genia's particular fantasies for Rochelle had started since Rochelle had changed in front of her that day the four of them went on vacation.

She recalled Rochelle's dark areolas and her cunt tightened at the mere thought of it. Genia recalled how the side of her arm had brushed Rochelle's soft breast and how it had sent tingles down her spine. The images of Rochelle's breast were clear in her mind. Genia would usually take every slight opportunity to feel Rochelle's assets. She wanted Rochelle to touch her breasts and every other parts of her body.

"Damn it," Genia muttered as another wave of arousal washed over her.

CHAPTER 2

"Wow!" Ben said as he stood at the doorway of his friend's apartment. It was his usual routine to leave his house in time and make a detour to his friend's place in the morning. The thought of the hot passionate sex they were about to have. They have started having the casual affair three years back. Ben recalled how Rochelle had propositioned him. At first, Ben had been worried because the thought of betraying his friend hadn't sat well with him. However, Rochelle had put his fears to rest when she had told him that, Stevie and her are in an open marriage they were into swinging. Ben had been amazed at this and he had let go off his inhibitions.

Ben had always liked the idea of an open marriage but had never brought it up with Genia because she was more of a conservative woman who had been raised to think the traditional way of a married is just a man and a woman. However, there was a condition to the relationship they shared and it was that neither Stevie or Genia would find out about them.

Although, Stevie and Rochelle had agreed to an open relationship, Ben didn't think it would be a bright idea for them to tell their partners about their affair. However, Ben had no idea that Stevie usually watched him fuck his wife, Stevie would watch them through hidden cameras all over the house. Stevie would stay hidden and jerked off to Ben fucking Rochelle. The sex was more pleasurable for Rochelle at the thought of Stevie watching her.

However, there was a particular fantasy she craved for.

Anticipation filled Ben as Rochelle sashayed towards him in her gown which barely reached her mid-thigh. He almost let out a deep groan as he stared at the fresh thighs of his friend's wife. Ben's eyes drifted to Rochelle's breast which looked like it would pop out of the gown she wore.

"Yes," Rochelle whispered as she reached where Ben stood. She wrapped her arms around his neck before she leaned in. Immediately, Ben slammed his lips to hers as he pulled her to himself until her breasts were cushioned against his chest. Rochelle's fingers went into his hair as she tried to get even more closer to his warmth. Ben guided Rochelle deeper into the living room before he shut the door with his foot. She laid on the sofa. He started sucking on her neck while Rochelle moaned.

Ben's hand went to Rochelle's bareback, and he rubbed it while still sucking on her neck. Rochelle shivered at this as her fingers grazed Ben's body her hand could reach. Rochelle soon discarded Ben's jacket before she tried to remove his shirt. However, this wasn't an easy task for her, as she could barely make any sense at the moment. Ben tried to discard Rochelle's clothing for a while, too, until he found the clasp holding her gown to her body.

He swiftly released the clasp and stopped kissing her neck long enough to remove her gown. Rochelle was now only clad in her panties as she panted heavily with desire. Rochelle hadn't worn a bra because it would have gone wrong with the dress she was wearing. Ben started raining kisses on her face before he moved to her chest area as his hands cupped her breast firmly. Rochelle moaned at this, but her moan grew louder as Ben covered one of her breasts with his mouth as he sucked.

"Oh my! Ben!" Rochelle screamed as she moaned while he kept sucking on her breast. Ben covered her body with his as he sucked her breast.

She tried removing his shirt again but failed miserably before Ben decided to help her out of her misery by removing his shirt after he ripped off the buttons. He directed his attention back to her other breast and started sucking hard on it. Rochelle moaned as her fingers went into Ben's hair while she held him closer to her breast. Her core was wet with desire at this point as she writhed beneath him. Her fingers tried to go between their bodies as she tried to unbuckle his belt. She was unsuccessful, as her hands weren't steady any longer.

Ben once again helped her as he released her breast and started trailing kisses down her stomach till, he reaches her panty line. Ben swiftly discarded his trousers until he was left in his briefs as he stood up from her body. He carried her and headed straight to the bedroom while she kissed his neck just like he had done earlier to her. They soon reached Rochelle's bedroom, and he gently placed her on the bed before he covered her body, with his as he kissed her passionately again. He trailed down once more after he stopped kissing her till, he got to her panty line again. He discarded her panties as he ripped through them while Rochelle gasped. He stared at her core for a brief moment with a hungry look before his mouth covered her.

"Be...Ben!" Rochelle screamed as she moaned at the contact of his lips with her core.

Ben groaned in pleasure as he started sucking her core hard while Rochelle writhed beneath him. He held her legs open as he devoured her core rapidly even when she instinctively tried to close her legs.

"Oh my goodness!" She screamed as Ben inserted two of his fingers into her while he still sucked her.

"Yes...ye..sss...that's it Ben!" Rochelle screamed as her body jerked while she orgasmed. Ben let her juice wash over him as he kept sucking her while her body calmed down from the orgasm. He soon raised himself up above her, and he was pleased with himself as he saw the look on Rochelle's face. She was completely sated while he grinned at this. He started kissing her again before his hand reached for his pants for protection. He soon, donned the condom after he swiftly discarded his briefs. He guided himself into her pussy as he stared straight into Rochelle's eyes.

He groaned out as he gently pried her opening with his dick.

"Oh my, Rochelle," He groaned once more as he found his way into her and felt her heat while Rochelle moaned as her hands wrapped around him to hold him closer to herself. Her fingers scraped his back as she was lost in the pleasure of having him fully inside her. Ben paused for a while after he had fully gained entrance as they tried to catch their breath before he started kissing every part of Rochelle's face he could reach. He started moving slowly in, and out of her.

"That's it bitch," Ben grunted into her ear. Rochelle liked hearing dirty words while she is being fucked. It intensified everything for her.

"Take that," Ben moaned as he kept thrusting in and out of her.

"Fuck!" Rochelle screamed as Ben increased his pace a bit. They both had their eyes barely open as they moaned. It became difficult for Ben to hold off his orgasm as the intensity of the pleasure increased. He kept thrusting until Rochelle screamed out in orgasm before he followed closely behind with a grunt.

Ben dislodged from Rochelle before she maneuvered their position until he was laying on the sofa and Rochelle was laying on top of him. They knew it was the beginning of their sex for the day. Ben was still thinking about various positions he would take her in. Rochelle stared directly at the hidden cameras and smiled. She imagined her husband jerking off. She wondered what it would feel like if he could join them and how intense it would be if Genia also joined. The mere thought of swinging partners made Rochelle's toes curl. Rochelle put all thoughts aside as she sat astride Ben to continue from where she had stopped.

CHAPTER 3

"Good evening dear," Rochelle greeted with a smile as she pulled Genia in for a hug. Genia and Ben had arrived at Rochelle and Stevie's place for dinner.

"Good evening Rochelle," Genia said with a small smile as she firmly pressed Rochelle against herself. Genia wanted to feel the weight of Rochelle's breast against hers. Unknown to her, Rochelle was enjoying the hug as much as Genia did. Rochelle was tempted to allow her palm reach out and grab Genia's ass. For a brief moment, Rochelle imagined fondling them. They pulled back after what seemed like eternity.

"Genia, it's good to have you here, and this dude," Stevie said with a smile as he opened his arms wide.

"Thank you," Genia said as she hugged Stevie. Stevie held her tightly and Rochelle smiled as she stared at both of them. She imagined them in another situation. A sexual one, where Stevie and Genia was kissing. Rochelle's eyes darkened with desire as they pulled back.

"Please, lead the way," Stevie said as he stepped aside with Rochelle to let Genia and Ben in.

"Thank you," Ben said as he wrapped his arm around Genia's waist and led her to the dining room. Stevie and Rochelle followed behind as it gave Rochelle the opportunity to stare at Genia's ass. Rochelle wished Genia was more open minded. Rochelle wanted Genia but knew that Genia wasn't into women unlike her. Rochelle occasionally had women too hence it was no new thing to her.

Genia and Rochelle took seat side by side while their husband faced them.

"How has it been with the both of you?" Rochelle asked as she served their meal.

"It has been good," Genia replied almost breathlessly. She wanted to reach out and trace Richelle's thigh. She wondered whether Rochelle's core was wet or not. Genia swallowed as she stole glances at Rochelle from the corner of her eyes. They started making small talks at the table while Rochelle and Genia barely paid attention. Rochelle smiled at Stevie in mischief as she raised her legs under the table until they met Stevie's dick through his clothes. Stevie smiled in mischief as he discreetly released his dick to give Rochelle access. Rochelle took the cue and caressed Stevie's dick with her foot.

Genia frowned when she noticed Stevie's darken while Rochelle had a mischievous smile on her face. Genia knew something was up with the couple but couldn't guess what it was. The meal continued with small talks before Genia excused herself to go to the restroom. Rochelle watched Genia leave and an idea popped in her head. She stood and excused herself from the table. Stevie gave her a look of disappointment because it meant Rochelle would stop pleasuring him in the time being. Rochelle made her way to the restroom and heard Genia doing her business.

"Genia, are you there?" She asked as she leaned against the door.

"Yes, I am. Give me a minute," Genia replied while Rochelle smiled. The door opened a few minutes later and Genia stepped out of the restroom.

"Is there a problem?" Genia asked auth a frown.

"I'm not sure if there is. I've been feeling some pains in my breasts and I don't know what could be the cause," Rochelle said.

"That's something. Have you visited your doctor?" Genia asked with alarmed eyes.

"I know I should. I only wanted to be sure that I'm not imagining these things. It could be an error on my part and I don't want to have Stevie worried as a result of this," Rochelle said.

"I'm going to go to my doctor, but first, all I ask is that, you give it a check for me," Rochelle said.

"Sure," Genia said and this pleased Rochelle.

"Okay, please follow me," Rochelle said and Genia followed her while she led the way. Rochelle led Genia to one of the rooms in the house.

"Okay, here we go," Rochelle said as she removed her top. Genia's eyes widened and she rapidly swallowed as Rochelle's breast came into view. Genia stared at Rochelle's round and full breast which looked like it was about to pop out of the bra she wore.

She was speechless when Rochelle unclasped her bra and her breast tumbled free.

"I don't know the exact point of the pain, you might have to look around," Rochelle said as she inwardly smiled when Genia stared at her breasts in awe.

Genia moved closer towards Rochelle and reached out to feel her breast. She was transfixed at the beauty and softness. Genia couldn't help herself as she softly pressed Rochelle's breast. Rochelle let out a soft moan at this with her eyes closed. Genia's breathing quickened as she raised her other palm to Rochelle's left breast.

"Do you think there is anything unusual with my breasts?" Rochelle asked with a sultry voice as she held Genia's gaze. Genia was tongue-tied and couldn't give a sound response. She shook her head instead as she felt Rochelle's breast with her palm.

"Are you sure about that? You can check the sides to ensure that nothing is out of place," Rochelle said whispered. At this, Genia started moving her fingers around until it reach Genia's areola. She couldn't resist the urge to pinch the nipples. Rochelle released another moan which excited Genia and encouraged her to pinch the other nipple. Genia couldn't believe that some her fantasies about Rochelle was playing out.

"Rochelle! Genia! Are you Okay?" Stevie called out from the hallway. At this the both of them sprang apart.

"I," Genia stammered as she tried to think of an explanation for what had happened.

"Its fine," Rochelle said with a reassuring smile.

"We are in here!" Rochelle called out as she tried to wear her bra.

"Okay, I'll take my leave," Genia said as she left the room.

"There you are. Where is Rochelle?" Stevie asked with a smile.

"She is in there," Genia said before she hurriedly returned to the dining room. Stevie watched as Genia left and knew something was up with her. He sauntered towards the room Rochelle was to get an explanation from her. She was rattled with what had happened between her and Rochelle. She had imagined it but had never thought the opportunity would present itself.

"Are you Okay?" Ben asked with a frown when Genia joined him at the table. She was still looking startled.

"Yes, I am," Genia said with a shy smile. She couldn't shake off the image of what had happened some minutes back. She wondered what would have happened if Stevie hadn't interrupted them. Stevie and Rochelle returned to the dining room later than expected. Unknown to Ben and Genia, Rochelle and Stevie had fucked while they had watched the footage of Genia caressing Rochelle's breast.

They joined the table and carried on like nothing had happened. Genia couldn't help herself as she stole glances at Rochelle all through the dinner. The only thing she could think about was the possibility of completing what they had started.

Genia and Ben left some hours later and returned to their apartment.

"I have to get something done in the hall," Genia said as they were about to call it a night.

"Okay, sweetheart," Ben said as he yawned and laid on the bed. Genia was pleased that Ben hadn't suggested that he escorted her. She had patiently waited all night to fantasize about what could have ended what she had started with Rochelle. Hence, she discreetly took her nine inches dick and headed out of the room. She made her way to one of the empty rooms in the house and shut the door.

Genia hurriedly unbuttoned her blouse. Then, she hurriedly moved to the empty bed after discarding her blouse. She laid on the bed before removing her panties. She kept her skirt on, she began rubbing the fat bulb head of the dildo across her pussy lips. Her cunt was wet, it made slick noises as the dildo slid into her centre.

Her knees parted more and more, allowing the erotic toy to have more access to her pussy. Its width pressed tightly against her moist folds. She popped a nipple beneath her bra. Her pussy grew wetter as the image of Rochelle's desirous look flooded her mind. It was Rochelle's face she tried to summon as the dildo sunk deep into her.

"Yes..." she moaned as she picked a rhythm up as she recalled Rochelle's moan. She was putting more and more inside her, feeling the toy cock hitting her favourite spots.

With her legs now spread eagle, Genia arched her back as she slammed the fat tip all the way in, before back out again. Her pussy was making smacking sounds as she felt a massive orgasm coming. She pinched her nipples the way she had pinched Rochelle's nipple. The sensation had her cumming all over the place. Cum shot out her pussy and ran all over hand and bed.

"Ahhh... Rochelle," she trimmored as her body released the pent-up tension in her pussy. With all 9 inches of the dildo deep, she fell asleep.

CHAPTER 4

Anticipation filled Genia as she parked her car in front of Stevie and Rochelle's house. It was three days after their last dinner. She had misplaced one of her earrings in their house the last time and it had been a perfect excuse for her to see Rochelle again.

Genia imagined given another opportunity to caress Rochelle's breasts. She smiled as she alighted form her car and made her way to the entrance. Genia knocked on the door for a brief moment and frowned when she got no response.

She sighed as she thought of the possibility of no one being at home.

She pressed the bell again before she realized that the door wasn't completely locked. Genia tentatively entered the quiet house.

"Rochelle!" She called out. Then, she heard it. The moans and groans that came from the direction of what Genia knew to be the bedroom. Genia's eyes widened at the thought of walking in in Stevie and Rochelle having sex. She was tempted to sneak a peek at them but thought otherwise. Genia was about to return to her car when she stopped on her tracks.

"What," She whispered as she walked towards the direction of one of the shoes carelessly discarded in the living room. She reached it and raised it. This was when she realized that it belonged to Ben. She recognized it because she had bought them for him as a birthday gift.

"What is?" She whispered before she stopped shouts while the moans and groans got louder.

"Could it be?" She whispered as she dropped the shoe. Her eyes darted around and this was when she noticed carelessly discarded trousers. Genia recalled it was the same pair Ben had worn before he had left the house earlier that morning.

"What the hell is going on?" She whispered to herself. She turned towards the direction where the moans and groans were coming from. She couldn't help herself as she started walking towards the room.

The moans and groans grew louder as she neared the room. They got clearer than before and Genia almost lost her head when she heard the familiar groans from Ben. She angrily opened the door and stood agape at the sight before her.

Ben laid on the bed while Rochelle sat astride him. However, she backed him, making her face the door.

"What!" Genia exclaimed. At this, Ben and Rochelle sprang apart. Genia couldn't help as her eyes moved in the direction of Rochelle's breast which swayed a bit.

Ben stared at Genia with wide eyes.

"I," He started to say.

"What the hell is going on here?" Genia asked with wide eyes.

"Genia," Rochelle said as she raised her palm. She was unashamed by her nudity while Ben stared at Genia in guilt. Genia glanced at Rochelle and her eyes strayed to her moist pussy. She wanted to be angry but she couldn't as she stared at Rochelle's breast. She wanted to scream at the both of them but stood transfixed. A part of her head wanted to lash out at the both of them for their betrayal while another part wanted to cross the gap between her and Rochelle and kiss her.

She knew the right thing would be to turn to leave but she couldn't. Rochelle knew the effect she had on Genia and moved. A moan almost escaped Genia's lips as she stared at Rochelle's breast.

"I'm sorry, I can explain," Ben said. At this point, he was out of the bed. Genia had been busy staring at Rochelle's breast that she didn't notice when he had put on his boxers.

"Explain, I'm intrigued to listen to what the explanation of this might be," Genia said as she briefly glanced at Ben's direction before she returned it to Rochelle's direction. Rochelle's eyes had darkened at this point and she darted her lips out to lick her lower lip. Genia wanted to be the one to taste Rochelle's lips. At this, Genia realized this was an opportunity to play out her fantasies about Rochelle.

"What you have done is terrible. I think Stevie needs to hear about this," Genia said barely removing her haze from Rochelle's breast.

"No, please he can't hear about this," Rochelle pretended like it mattered. She knew Stevie was currently watching all of them.

"Is that so? There is a price to pay for that," Genia said as she sauntered towards the bed.

"Price? What is it? Name it and you will have it done," Ben hurriedly said. He was agitated.

"There is one thing I've craved for a long time. I want to know how it feels," Genia said while Ben frowned.

"You can have everything as long as you forgive me and you don't mention this to Stevie," Ben said and this brought a smile on Genia's face.

"Good, you won't mind if I replace you on the bed with Rochelle while you watch," Genia said and Ben stared at her in shock. Never in his wildest imagination did he think Genia would make such a request.

"You want to replace me on the bed, with her?" Ben asked to be sure he had heard correctly.

"Yes, I want Rochelle to fuck me," Genia said as she glanced at Rochelle.

"Do you have a problem with that?" She asked as she held Rochelle's gaze before she returned it to Ben. Anticipation filled Rochelle at this. She recalled what had happened between them three days back. At the time, she had wanted to tease Genia. She hadn't guessed Genia would enjoy it so much she would want a repeat of it.

"Genia? Is this because of what you saw? Is this for revenge, I promise," Ben started to say but Genia held up her palm.

"My life doesn't revolve around you. I want to know what it would feel like to have a woman," Genia said.

"I'm sure Rochelle would find a way around it," Genia said with a smile. She was nervous about her first soon to be lesbian experience but felt this was the only chance she had.

"No, I've been with a number of women," Rochelle said.

"You see that we have no problem," Genia said as she held Ben's gaze.

"Are you sure?" Ben asked for the last time and Genia arched her brows. Ben took that as a cue to go to the only chair in the room. He couldn't believe what he was about to witness.

Genia returned her attention to Rochelle and became confused about what to do. Her courage dissipated and Rochelle knew this. Rochelle smiled before she got closer to Genia. She made an internal vow to give Genia her most memorable lesbian experience.

Rochelle smiled as she wrapped her palm around the back of Genia's neck. Genia's breathing increased as Rochelle lowered her lips to Genia's lips. Genia closed her eyes as their lips touched. They let out a moan. Genia wrapped her arms around Rochelle's neck and pulled her closer. She parted her lips to allow

Rochelle gain entrance. Another moan escaped her as their tongues battled. Genia felt the desire which made her toe curl. She ran her fingers through Rochelle's hair as she lost all sense of time and place. She forgot that Ben was watching them. Ben gasped as he saw the both women in front of him. His dieing erection started growing as the image before him was the hottest thing he had ever seen.

Rochelle pulled back and smiled when she saw Genia's dazed expression. Genia grabbed the back of Rochelle's neck before she slammed her lips to it. The kiss was faster than the first one. Their tongues duelled while Rochelle's palm reached out until he fondled Genia's ass. Genia let out a gasp when Rochelle released her lips. Her eyes were tilted in desire as Rochelle lowered her head and sucked on her neck. Genia let out a low moan before Rochelle returned her lips to hers. Genia reached out as her palm caressed Rochelle's body until it landed on her bare ass. Genia pulled and pressed Rochelle's ass while they moaned into each other's mouth.

They ignored the groan that escaped Ben's lips as he watched them make out.

Rochelle released Genia's lips and hurriedly grabbed the gown she wore. She discarded it in a swift second. She smiled as she hurriedly unleashed her bra until Genia was left in her panties.

Rochelle cupped Genia's breast immediately as they were free. She pulled and pressed the breasts before she lowered her head until she captured one of the nipples in her mouth.

"Ahhh!" Genia screamed as Rochelle sucked one of her breasts. Genia was mindless as Rochelle sucked. Rochelle's fingers railed to her panties as she touched her pussy. She released the first breast with a pop before she moved to the second one.

"Yesss," Genia moaned in pleasure as her palm held Rochelle's head to her lips.

Rochelle released the other breast before Genia lowered her head to Rochelle's nipple. Genia let out a moan as Rochelle's nipple filled her mouth. It was the exact way she had imagined. Rochelle moaned as Genia sucked one of her breasts while she lightly pinched the other breast. Rochelle moaned as the intense pleasure hit her pussy.

Rochelle pulled Genia away from her breast before she slightly pushed her until she laid on her back. And begun to trailed kisses down Genia's stomach to her pussy which was still hidden beneath her panties. Rochelle smiled as her fingers trailed across Genia's pussy lips which made her even wetter. She removed Genia's panties while she held her gaze. At this point Ben had his dick out in the open while he slowly stroked it.

Rochelle smiled as she slowly discarded Genia's panties. She held Genia's gaze as she brought her panties to her nose and inhaled.

"You smell delicious," Rochelle said while Genia watched her with glazed eyes. Rochelle lowered her head until she was face to face with Genia's wet hot core.

"Ohhh!" Genia screamed as Rochelle covered her pussy with her lips. Genia's fingers went into Rochelle's hair as she tried to hold her head closer. Rochelle gave no mercy to Genia as she sucked her pussy hard. Genia screamed to the top of her lungs as Rochelle parted her labia and sucked her clitoris. Genia couldn't help the scream that tore from her throat as the pleasures took her over.

Rochelle was relentless, as Genia tried to even her breathing. She kept sucking Genia while she inserted one finger into her vagina. Rochelle tried moving her finger in and out of Genia while she sucked her pussy. Rochelle let out a groan as she felt Genia's heat. She increased the fingers to two and Genia started building up the second time. Rochelle increased the fingers to three while she increased the pace of how she sucked her clitoris. Genia was on the edge when Rochelle lightly but her numb. Another scream tore from Genia's lips as she orgasmed.

Rochelle smiled as she grabbed the dildo which laid on the drawer near the bed. Genia hadn't noticed it earlier. She watched with a dazed expression as Rochelle switched on the dildo. It was bigger that Genia's dildo. Genia was weak as she watched Rochelle guide the dildo to her pussy.

"Shit!" Genia screamed as she tried to move away when Rochelle rubbed the vibrating dildo on her clit. It sent different sensations down her spine while Rochelle held her down. Rochelle inserted the dildo in Genia's pussy.

"Oh," Genia moaned as Ben increased the pace, he used to stroke his dick.

Rochelle lowered her head and covered Genia's pussy lips with her mouth as she fucked her hard with the dildo. It wasn't long before Genia screamed out as she orgasmed the third time. At this point, she was boneless and could do nothing as Rochelle hurriedly moved until she sat on her face. Rochelle's pussy lips were directly to Genia's lips while she faced Genia's pussy. They were in a form of sixty-nine position. Genia wasted no time as she started sucking Rochelle's pussy. Rochelle let out a low moan as she covered Genia's pussy with her lips. She inserted the vibrator in her once more while she sucked.

At this point, Genia's fingers trailed to Rochelle's ass while she sucked. Their moans filled the room while Ben got closer to his orgasm. Rochelle let out a loud groan when Genia pried her ass hole with her finger. Rochelle started grinding when Genia started moving her finger in and out of her while she sucked Rochelle's pussy. The both of them were lost at this point.

Genia became undone for the fourth time when Rochelle bit her clit. She jolted in orgasm and as a result she bit Rochelle's clit. They came together while Ben grunted out his release. Rochelle got up and smiles at both Ben and Genia and said, "We should do this again with all four of us, how do next Saturday sound."

Naughty Hotwife Swingers Experience

First Time MFFM Sex
Taboo Cheating Marriage Romance Short Story

Adult Erotic Lesbian Fiction
KATE KAT

Kindle Edition
Copyright 2021 Khelan Publishing
Published by Khelan Publishing
License Notes: This ebook is licensed for your personal enjoyment only. This ebook may not be re-sold or given away to other people. If you would like to share this ebook with another person, please purchase an additional copy for each person you share it with. If you're reading this book and did not purchase it, or it was not purchased for your use only, then you should return and purchase your own copy. Thank you for respecting the hard work of this author.
Khelan Publishing Printing March 2021
5 4 3 2 1

~

All characters in this book have no existence outside the imagination of the author and have no relation whatsoever to anyone bearing the same name or names. They are not even distantly inspired by any individual known or unknown to the author, and all incidents are pure inventions of fiction.

Table of Content
Naughty HotWife Swingers Experience

> CHAPTER 1
> CHAPTER 2
> CHAPTER 3
> CHAPTER 4

CHAPTER 1

"Yes baby! Oh my goodness! Yes!" Genia screamed as Ben slammed his cock into her. They were on the couch at their apartment fucking each other's brains out. Ben wanted to reinstate his ability to pleasure Genia in her head. It was a week after, he had been forced to watch Rochelle fuck her. In actual fact, Ben didn't feel like he had been forced to watch his wife fuck his best friend's wife. The memory of how hot the both of them had been on the bed made him increase the furious pace of his thrusts.

"Yes! Ben!" Genia screamed as he raised her legs and allowed them rest on his shoulder. Although, he hadn't raised the topic with Genia after the incident. He couldn't help but wonder if she would want a repeat of what had happened that day. He wanted to watch the two women fuck themselves while he jerked off. Ben opened his eyes and watched Genia's dazed expression whole she let out load moans. He watched as she parted her lips and the pink tip of her mouth came out.

"You're going to be the death of me," Ben groaned as he dropped one of his palm to cover Genia's pussy. He started stroking her clitoris with his thumb.

"Ben! Fuck Yes! Fuck me baby!" Genia squealed and Ben gritted his teeth as he increased his pace with hard, deep strokes. Ben closed his eyes as the memory of jerking off flooded his mind. At this point, he wished Genia hadn't placed a rule of not joining her and Rochelle because it was what he imagined. He imagined fucking Genia while Rochelle sat in her face. Ben imagined, Genia moaning under the both of them. He dropped his other hand towards her breast. Ben, slightly tweaked Genia's nipple while he didn't cease in rubbing her pussy with his other hand. He kept slamming into her and felt Genia tightened. He gave a satisfied smile because he knew Genia was close.

"Fuck!" Genia screamed before she gave into her orgasm. Ben closed his eyes and gritted his teeth to keep himself from coming when he felt her tighten around his dick. She was pushing him close to his orgasm but he wasn't ready to let up. Hence, he reduced the pace of his thrust while Genia clenched and clenched around his dick.

"Ben," Genia moaned as she finally eased.

"Genia," Ben moaned as he started the ride all over again. He couldn't get enough of his wife. Ben recalled how she had knocked him out when she had asked that Rochelle fucked her. He had wanted her to be more open but he hadn't expected that she harboured inner fantasies until that day. Ben watched Genia with a desirous look as he thrust in and out of her. He wondered how open Genia was ready to get. He wondered what other sexual fantasies she had in her head. He was more than ready to fulfil them. However, Ben hadn't broached the topic because it would mean they would have a discussion about how he had been cheating on her with Rochelle. Genia hadn't said anything since that day and he wondered if it was her way of trying to forget about the whole thing which had happened. Ben was puzzled about why she would want to forget something as beautiful as that moment with Rochelle. He recalled how Genia had squirted multiple times all over Rochelle's face. Genia didn't usually squirt for him. He wondered if he could fuck her until she squirted. He felt empowered by the challenge to watch Genia lose control. He wanted her juice all over them and he was determined to get it.

"Ben! Yes! Right there!" Genia moaned as Ben angled his hips until he was hitting Genia sideways. He gritted his teeth and threw his head back when Genia became impossibly tighter. Her screams rose and Ben knew he had finally found the spot. He slammed his dick into her pussy as her screams sounded like music into his ears.

"Ben! Harder! I want it harder!" She screamed as Ben grabbed her hips to firmly hold her while he fired away with hard thrusts.

"Baby," Ben gasped as he felt a sizzling feeling down his spine. He knew it was a matter of time before his control would snap. However, he was determined to make the most of the moment as he increased his pace.

"Genia love," He grunted as her fingers grabbed his palm which were around his waist. Genia mumbled incoherent words but he was far gone to make sense of them. Ben slightly opened his mouth as Genia's pussy grew tighter around his girth.

"You have the sweetest pussy sweetheart," Ben moaned.

"Yes baby!" Genia screamed as Ben turned her around without dislodging himself from her body. She wondered how he had been able to achieve that feat but was unable to think too deep into it as Ben resumed the pace of his thrust. The room reeked of their sex and sweat but neither of them minded.

Perspiration covered the both of them as the sound of Ben's dick slamming into Genia's pussy filled the air. He thrust his whole dick into her while one of his fingers went to her pussy. He toyed with her clitoris while he never eased on his pace.

"I'm close Ben!" Genia exclaimed and Ben gritted his teeth. He was also close but couldn't let the words out because he believed he wouldn't be able to hold back from releasing after that.

Ben removed his palm from Genia's pussy and grabbed her hips. Her tight asshole beckoned to him and moved the fingers which had been at her pussy to the spot. Genia jerked forward like she was trying to move away from his touch. However, she couldn't create much distance as Ben firmly held her hips. He watched with dazed expression as his wet finger toyed with Genia's asshole.

"Oh Ben!" Genia screamed as he parted her asshole with one of his fingers. He allowed only the tip of his middle finger to enter her asshole while he continued slamming into her. He was starting to think of how he would have her ass after they came down from the height of pleasure they were at that moment. He smiled when Genia's asshole clasped around his fingers like it didn't want to release it. It wanted to suck his finger in and this caused Ben to grunt as he imagined her asshole trying to suck his dick in.

"Ben!" Genia screamed as she rested her head on the pillows. At this time she angled herself until her ass was up for Ben's thrust while the lower part of her body rested on the bed. Ben groaned as he stared at Genia's round ass. He couldn't help himself as he raised his palm and gave her ass a slight slap. She squealed and Ben gritted his teeth. He gave her other cheek a slap and Genia started thrusting back her ass to meet up with his thrust. Ben felt bliss as he felt a sharp sensation in the lower part of his spine. He was determined that they would enjoy the whole moment.

"Genia,!" He grunted when he felt himself get closer to the edge. His finger's went to Genia's pussy once more before he started slamming hard and deep into her.

"Fuck Yes! I want it like that! Ben! Give it to me! Oh my goodness!" Genia screamed while Ben tried to hold onto his self-control. She clenched her fingers on the bedspread and didn't care about it getting it torn as she was now mindless with pleasure. Genia imagined Rochelle on the bed with both of them. She imagined her lapping at her pussy while Ben fucked her. She imagined Ben fuck Rochelle while she sucked her as well. Her eyes widened as she wondered where the thought had come from. Genia had been unable to forget about the experience with Rochelle since the day it had happened. She wanted a repeat of it but she couldn't ask Ben for it. She recalled the condition which had enabled her to have an experience with Rochelle.

"Fuck!" Genia screamed as she snapped out of her thoughts when Ben thrust two fingers into her asshole. It hurt her a bit and she felt a tingling sensation before it eased.

"Yes baby! Come for me baby! Give me your juice!" Ben screamed as he slammed hard into Genia. Genia felt like she saw stars at that moment.

Ben grunted with satisfaction when he felt Genia squirted around his dick. He groaned out as he kept on thrusting into her. His orgasm knocked him out of his breath and he released with loud grunt. He jerked against Genia as spurts and spurts of his come filled her. He felt his strength desert him as he leaned against Genia's back. Genia's strength had also dissipated and she laid on the bed while Ben laid over her. He enjoyed the feeling of being enclosed in her tight pussy for a few seconds before he dislodged himself and laid beside Genia. Genia weakly turned until she laid on her back beside Ben. They both stared at the ceiling while they tried to catch their breath.

Genia felt satisfied but she felt there was something they were still missing. She thought about Rochelle and couldn't help but imagine what it would be like if she had joined her and Ben. Genia frowned when she realized where her thoughts were drifting towards. It felt like her experience with Rochelle had opened up many things within her. The problem was that she had no idea how much of her dark desires had been opened.

CHAPTER 2

"Good morning sir," Alicia Ben's PA greeted as he matched towards his office. He had started going in early for work since the day Genia had caught him on bed with Rochelle. Although, Genia hadn't spoken about it, he had felt it was best if he ended things with Rochelle. Rochelle had tried reaching out to him but he hadn't been able to bring himself to continue their affair because he didn't know what Genia's take was on it. Although, Genia didn't act like anything had happened, Ben wasn't ready to push his luck by continuing. He missed having Rochelle but he couldn't risk Stevie catching them.

"Good morning," Ben said without paying attention to her. She opened her mouth to say something but Ben's thoughts were clouded. He opened his office and it took a few minutes before he noticed it wasn't empty.

"Hello Ben," Rochelle said with a smile as she turned on the chair, she sat to face him. Ben swallowed when he took in Rochelle. He stared at the lushness of her breast which was open.

"She insisted on waiting for you in your office. I tried explaining," Alicia mumbled with an apologetic look. At this, Ben realized Alicia was in the office with them. He turned towards her as Rochelle said;

"I'm sure, he wouldn't mind. Isn't that correct?" She asked as she fixed her gaze on Ben.

"Please leave us Alicia," Ben said as he nodded towards her direction. Alicia rapidly nodded her head before she left the office. Ben sighed as he returned his attention towards Rochelle after Alicia left.

"Rochelle," Ben said as he walked towards her.

"It's been a while Ben. I waited for you at the apartment but you didn't show up," Rochelle said as she stood. Ben gasped when he saw the outfit she was wearing. She had a tight gown which barely reached her mid thighs. Her breasts were pushed forward and it looked like they would spill out from the dress.

"Rochelle," Ben said as he made his way to his chair while he tried to ignore the invitation of her breast beckoning to him. He sat while Rochelle smiled as she watched him. Rochelle knew it was because of what had happened between her and Genia. She knew he was scared of continuing what was between them because he was scared that Genia would catch them again. Rochelle was sure that what had happened between her and Genia wasn't abhorrent to Ben. She knew this because she had watched the video with Stevie and had seen the pleasure on his face while she had been fucking Genia. She recalled that he had kept releasing while he had watched them.

Rochelle felt a tingling sensation between her thighs when she recalled how Stevie had fucked her hard while watching the video. This was after they had left. That day had easily joined one of her memorable days. In fact, she wanted a repeat of it. However, she wanted it to involve Ben and Stevie as well.

There was a little problem as Ben had stopped coming over to her apartment. She had thought he would be back after a few days but she had been wrong when Ben hadn't showed up after one week. She had hoped that they would see each other in their usual dinners but she had been wrong when Genia nor Ben had showed up. She had decided to take the bull by the horn by coming to his office.

"Ben," Rochelle said as she gave him the sultry look, she knew would have an effect on him. She was right as she watched him inhale as he watched her from where he sat. Rochelle smiled as she assisted towards him. Her thighs rubbed against each other and she almost moaned when the friction made her bare pussy wetter. She imagined how Ben would feel like when he found out she had nothing under her dress. Rochelle felt a thrill run through her as she watched Ben's eyes darken as his gaze rested on her thighs. Rochelle wanted him with a strong intensity. The need had increased and she had no idea if it was due to the days they had spent apart. However, there was something knew for Rochelle. It was the fact that he wanted both Genia and Ben. Although, they had pulled back Rochelle wondered if it was due to the fact Ben was scared of Stevie finding out. It amused her that they were worried about Stevie when Stevie was aware of all that was happening.

"I've been calling you but you've been ignoring my calls," Rochelle said as she stopped beside Ben. Ben tried to distract himself by staring straight ahead. He tried not to stare at Rochelle's thigh but his effort was fruitless as he found his gaze drifting towards her thighs.

"You know the reason. Genia caught us and by some miracle she took it well. What would have happened if it was Stevie?" Ben said as he forced his eyes to rest on Rochelle's face.

"It wouldn't have made much difference," Rochelle said as she shrugged. Ben frowned at this.

"Trust me Stevie would have gone berserk about this," Ben said with wide eyes.

"Don't be so sure about that," Rochelle said as she chuckled while she stretched her palm until it rested on Ben's forearm.

"What do you mean?" Ben asked with a puzzled expression.

"That's beside the point. Genia enjoyed that day and I'm sure she wouldn't complain if we continue. If she wants us to have another moment like that day you can tell her I'm always available," Rochelle said as she trailed her fingers on Ben's exposed wrist.

Ben clenched his fist to refrain himself from reaching out and pulling Rochelle unto his laps.

"We can't take that risk," Ben said with clenched teeth.

"What risk? This is us having fun," Rochelle said as she stared at Ben. She had planned with Stevie that she was going to try and convince Ben into another sexual experience between her, Genia and him. The plan was that Stevie would join them in the middle of that. However, with what she was seeing showed that it would be a difficult task to convince Ben. Hence, she had to settle for the other option Stevie had suggested.

"Anyways, that's not why I came," Rochelle said even though her pussy screamed for some sexual touches. However, she decided that she would be patient for the better plan ahead.

Ben released a sigh of relief that Richelle had dropped the topic. However, deep down he wanted to pull her closer and kiss her. He wanted to lay her across the table and fuck her brains out like he usually did.

"We are going to be having a party. You and Rochelle are invited," She said.

"A party?" Ben asked with a puzzled expression.

"Yes. You didn't come over for dinner and Stevie thinks something is up. Hence, I suggested a party," Rochelle said.

"Oh, I see," Ben said.

"Yes, please tell Genia. It's this Friday. We'll be expecting the both of you and don't be late," Rochelle said. Ben stared at Rochelle for a while. He could see the mischievous look she had on her face and wondered what the cause of it was.

He knew he was up to something but couldn't pinpoint what it was. Rochelle could see Ben calculating but she didn't wait to find out what he was thinking before she leaned in and placed a kiss on his forehead.

"See you at the party," Rochelle said before she left the office. Ben clenched his fist as he inhaled the sweet fragrance of her perfume. He hoped that Stevie wouldn't find out about them.

CHAPTER 3

"We aren't too early, are we?" Genia asked with wide eyes as she faced Rochelle and Stevie. She was standing beside Ben and they were at Rochelle and Stevie's apartment.

"No, you aren't," Stevie said with a smile.

"We shifted the party to tomorrow. Hence, we informed the others about it. It must have slipped my mind to send you the message," Rochelle said with a smile. Genia relaxed at this but she couldn't help but stare at Rochelle. Memories of kissing her lips, sucking her breast and her pussy flooded her mind.

"I see, we should be on our way," Ben said.

"Nonsense, there is no way you will be returning now that you are here," Stevie said.

"Are you sure?" Ben said as he tried to keep his gaze from Rochelle. She wore a similar gown to the one she had worn when she had been to his office some days back. However, the one she was currently wearing was transparent and he could see through the black gown.

"Of course. Let's have a drink," Stevie said as he wrapped his arm around Ben and led him to the kitchen. Ben was nervous and hoped that his worst fears hadn't come through. He wondered of Genia had told Stevie about what had happened and now his friend was trying to torture him.

They got to the kitchen and Stevie served them the drink.

"We'll be right back guys," Rochelle announced as she entered the kitchen.

"Okay," Stevie said with a smile before she turned and left. Ben couldn't help his eyes as they glued on Rochelle's lips. He could see her ass and it looked like Rochelle wasn't wearing anything under the gown.

"You like?" Stevie started. At this, Ben realized Rochelle had left. He cringed when he realized Stevie had caught him staring.

"It's not what you think," Ben hurriedly said.

"Come on. I'm asking for your opinion," Stevie said as he drank part of his scotch.

"What's not to like," Ben said as he tried to shrug it off.

"I know especially when her pussy squeezes tightly on my dick. I wonder of Genia's pussy feels the same way," Stevie said and Ben eyes widened at this.

"What are you saying?" Ben slurred.

"I know about you and Rochelle," Stevie said as he shrugged while Ben tensed.

"Stevie," Ben said as he started to apologize. He was surprised when Stevie burst into laughter.

"Calm down man. I've known for a long time. In fact, it makes my day to see the both of you fuck. It builds my anticipation for after you leave because I get to fuck her harder," Stevie said and Ben's eyes widened.

"Before you cut in. Rochelle knows I watch the both of you fuck," Stevie said with a shrug.

"She does?" Ben asked with a bewildered expression.

"Yes. We are open with our relationship," Stevie said with a grin.

"Then, Genia stunned me with her request. Hence, the reason the idea of swinging between the both of you came up," Stevie said.

"Swinging? You mean exchanging our partners?" Ben asked.

"Yes, it sounds mind-blowing. Rochelle and I do it from time to time," Stevie said.

"Stevie," Ben whispered. He was trying to process what Stevie was saying when he heard Genia's loud moan.

"I see they started before us," Stevie said as he stood. Ben stood with him and walked with Stevie towards the place the sound was coming from. Ben swallowed when they reached a room and found Rochelle and Genia kissing. They were both naked. They released each other's lips before they faced them.

"We are waiting," Rochelle said with a grin. Stevie chuckled as he hurriedly discarded his clothes. Ben took that as a cue to do the same. Stevie made how ray to the bed to Rochelle's side.

Rochelle's mouth met his as they started kissing. Stevie's hand slid slowly up her naked thigh, as their tongues battled.

Ben watched as Stevie's hand travelled between Rochelle's legs and cupped her pussy.

Ben could feel his dick hardened while Genia's breathing became laboured as she stared at Stevie and Rochelle. Ben moved to join Genia on the bed and he wrapped his arm around her. Ben pulled her closer and they started kissing.

Stevie broke the embrace.

"Do you mind swinging with them?" he said as he held Genia's gaze. She had desire in her eyes.

"Rochelle told me how it would be fun. Let's do this," Genia whispered.

CHAPTER 4

"That's it," Stevie said as he pulled back from kissing Rochelle.

Genia felt no jealousy, but what came next shocked her.

Genia watched as Stevie cupped his meaty circumcised dick which was about nine inches long. Rochelle got on her knees before him and took him in her mouth

Genia watched as Rochelle sucked Stevie and she felt her pussy grow moist. She was turned on as Ben tweaked her nipple with his fingers.

Ben's cock became harder as he watched Rochelle's lips suck tenderly on Stevie's dick. Rochelle and Stevie had Genia and Ben entranced in what they were doing.

"Do you want to join?" Rochelle asked as she glanced in their direction.

Genia couldn't speak, but her eyes told it all.

Ben kissed her deep, letting his hands roam to her petite frame. A slight moan escaped from Genia's mouth when Ben's finger covered her mound.

Genia closed her eyes at the sensation before Ben whispered;

"Keep looking at them,"

Genia opened her eyes before she returned her attention to Stevie and Rochelle.

She watched as Rochelle began deep throating all of Stevie's cock. Genia saw the massive sized balls hanging between Stevie's legs. She raised her head and found Stevie was looking right at her.

"It's okay if you want to join in," Ben whispered in her ears when he saw what had Rochelle's attention.

He was now behind her and held her by the hips. His hands were rubbing the area beneath her belly button.

"Ben," she whispered.

Ben moaned when he felt Genia's soaking pussy.

Ben pressed his dick into her backside. He was turned on by everything going on. He groaned when he heard Rochelle's sexy moans and stared at her sexy ass.

"How about you give Rochelle a little help," Ben told her.

Genia was shocked and looked at him. But he only smiled, as he now had his cock in his hand.

Genia was transfixed with lust at the sight of Stevie's cock. She almost could feel her mouth drooling, feeling the strong urge to kiss it and stroke it and just be a naughty girl with it.

"Come on," he said, stroking himself as he released her.

Genia made her way towards Rochelle and Stevie. Rochelle was now sucking the sides of his thick cock, and rubbing her nails against his inner thighs, when she saw Genia, she smiled and released Stevie's dick.

"Have fun sweetheart," Rochelle said with a smile.

Genia got down on her knees and took Stevie's big cock into her mouth, slowly moving her head back and forth as Stevie's cock parted her soft lips then disappeared inside her mouth before slowly pulling back out. Stevie picked up his pace as Genia's mouth started to get wetter with her spit and by this time both of them where moving in tandem as Stevie's dick grows even harder.

Rochelle maneuvered her way closer to Genia and started rubbing her breast, while she sucked her husband. Stevie was in bliss and he stiffened as his dick explode his hot load into Genia's welcoming mouth. Stevie remained stiff for a moment except for a few erratic jerks before slowly pulling his flaccid cock out of Genia's mouth.

Ben watched as Rochelle kissed Genia licking up the rest of Stevie's load off her lips and the scene made him almost come on himself. There was something hot about seeing the two women kissing so passionately.

It lasted a few moments before Rochelle returned to the blowjob. She asked Genia to come closer and continued doing what she liked with Stevie's cock. Ben looked at Genia who slowly covered Stevie's cockhead into her mouth once again.

Ben's cock entered Rochelle's hot cunt, he groaned at the feeling of feeling her hot pussy again. Ben smiled when he noticed Rochelle had control of her inner walls, as she gripped him on every stroke. Genia couldn't believe how thick and hard Stevie's cock had gotten, after cumming not only moments ago.

She slurped on the tip, and moaned as seed of precum appeared. Genia was now sucking Stevie's balls and moaning. Genia moan at the thought of having Stevie's big dick deep inside her. It made her own pussy ache.

Genia got up and crawled onto Stevie.

Stevie watched her with a smile knowing she needed him to fuck her good. Stevie lifted up Genia and tried to slide her down on top of his fat cock but had trouble to fit him inside her. She used her hand to guide his dick but he was just too thick. Finally, after many efforts, they forced his thick cock inside of her small hole, stretching her to accommodate his massive size. Genia could feel Stevie's cock rubbing against her narrow walls as he slowly intruded her tight cunt. Genia used her hand to pull apart her butt cheeks an attempt to stretch her vagina open some more to allow Stevie's nine-inch cock to fill her up totally.

"Oh my god!" Genia cried as Stevie's cock fully entered her. Ben was turned on seeing her take Stevie's cock so deep.

Once she was adjusted somewhat, Genia started to ride Stevie's cock and almost immediately she could feel his cock rubbing against her G-spot with every rock her hips made.

"Oh Yes!" Genia cried out, as she rocked and pushed down hard on his dick, her cunt getting even wetter, Stevie's cock milking her of all her pussy juice. He captured one of her breasts in his mouth and started sucking on it greedily.

Genia's pace got faster, lost in bliss as she felt her body on the edge, he began stroking her as she rode him, each stroke he made drove Genia wild. She continued slamming herself against him as she screamed, "Fuck I'm cumming …"

A wave of juice squirted out of her coating Stevie's cock and lower abdomen

"Ben closed his eyes as the pleasure of seeing Genia with Stevie was getting too much for him. He started slamming into Rochelle like his life depended on it.

"I want you to cum down my throat," Rochelle asked as she turned to face Ben.

"I wanna taste your dick. It's been too long," she continued. Ben nodded as he kept slamming into her. Stevie also slammed hard into Genia. Genia and Rochelle's moan filled the room while the men grunted in pleasure.

Ben removed his dick from Rochelle's pussy when he realized he was close to coming. Rochelle took that as a cue as she swiftly turbid until she faced him. She started rubbing his ball before she took his dick down her throat. The sensation sent chills up Ben's spine before he knew he would bus his load soon, Rochelle's tongue tickled him to a hard nut.

"Fuck!" Ben grunted as he started releasing his sperm into her mouth. Rochelle was going to be the death of him.

Stevie was still fucking Genia and she was rapidly growing closer to another orgasm. He flipped her over on the bed and slammed into her while she was spread beneath him. She began moaning loudly as her orgasm hit her. Stevie followed behind as he withdrew his cock and shot cum all over her stomach.

Stevie began eating Genia's pussy. His tongue felt good sliding, in and out of her, and on her clit.

"Fuck!" Genia screamed out.

Rochelle and Ben maneuvered themselves until Ben lay on the bed and she sat astride him. His dick was still hard and Rochelle continued from where they had stopped as she covered his dick with her pussy. She rode pleasing herself while Ben used her big breasts as leverage. Rochelle screamed as Ben slammed into her while Genia was screaming from jolts of pleasures ripping through her from the onslaught of Stevie's tongue.

Stevie raised himself as he slammed into Genia. A grunt tore from her throat at this before she realized Ben was beside her. Ben guided his cock into his wife's mouth, Genia felt free and enjoyed sucking her husband's cock, while Stevie fucked her. She wondered where Rochelle was but didn't pay much attention to it as the two men slammed into her.

Stars exploded behind her eyes as she started screaming when her orgasm hit her. Her scream was muffled with Ben's dick in her mouth.

Ben grunted as he released in her mouth while Stevie removed his dick and released on her stomach the second time.

"That's it baby," Ben whispered as he used his dick to tap Genia's lips. Genia felt overload on pleasure as she laid between the men.

The two men left her to recuperate when she noticed them advance towards Rochelle. She watched with a dazed expression as they pounced on her. Genia knew it was going to be a long night.

Printed in Dunstable, United Kingdom

68317783R10077